"I'm Roland."

"Angel." He lifted his brows at her reply, and she added, "My name. A nickname I've grown used to. My full name is Angelica Mornay."

"It suits you. Pretty name for a pretty dame."

His casual compliment left her ill at ease, and she looked down, snapping her purse shut.

"Did I say something wrong?"

Before she could respond, the waiter returned to the table with their orders. "If there will be anything else, Mr. Piccoli, please do not hesitate to ask."

"Bring the lady a sandwich as well. I'm sure she must be hungry."

The shock of hearing his name struck Angel like an unexpected dousing of icy water; she couldn't think to respond or refuse. A kaleidoscope of startling facts twisted inside her mind, making her dizzy.

Roland Piccoli! Grandson of the notorious gangster Vittorio Piccoli. . .who dispensed with his enemies as casually as she dispensed with a pair of damaged stockings. No wonder he seemed familiar when she saw him at her aunt's! His face had been plastered in the society pages a month ago, a blushing debutante on his arm, who the article had said was his fiancée. And Angel had run across his ~~path~~ not once but twice. . . .

Walking twice into the ~~same~~ ~~diner~~.

PAMELA GRIFFIN lives in Texas and divides her time among family, church activities, and writing. She fully gave her life to the Lord in 1988 after a rebellious young adulthood and owes the fact that she's still alive today to an all-loving and forgiving God and a mother who prayed that her wayward daughter would come "home." Pamela's main goal in writing Christian romance is to encourage others through entertaining stories that also heal the wounded spirit. Please visit Pamela at www.Pamela-Griffin.com.

Books by Pamela Griffin

HEARTSONG PRESENTS

Don't miss out on any of our super romances. Write to us at the following address for information on our newest releases and club information.

Heartsong Presents Readers' Service
PO Box 721
Uhrichsville, OH 44683

Or visit www.heartsongpresents.com

In Search
of a Memory

Pamela Griffin

Heartsong Presents

To all those searching who have lost something special and to all those wishing to find a better way and the truth, this is for you. Many thanks to my critique partners, Theo, Therese, and my mother. Without you guys, I would be lost. And to my Lord and Savior, Jesus Christ, who found this lost lamb and brought her home, to Him I owe everything.

A note from the Author:
I love to hear from my readers! You may correspond with me by writing:

> **Pamela Griffin**
> **Author Relations**
> **PO Box 721**
> **Uhrichsville, OH 44683**

ISBN 978-1-60260-698-2

IN SEARCH OF A MEMORY

All scripture quotations are taken from the King James Version of the Bible.

Our mission is to publish and distribute inspirational products offering exceptional value and biblical encouragement to the masses.

PRINTED IN THE U.S.A.

one

Lanville, New York, 1935

Angel Mornay couldn't pinpoint why she felt uneasy, but every nerve inside screamed out a warning to keep away from this man. He was definitely not the typical sort to appear at their door.

The tall, dark stranger in the black suit continued to stare, ignoring her two cousins. "I'm pleased I could be of some assistance." He tipped his felt fedora. "Ladies." At once he moved away, his fluid stride a strange mix of confidence and caution.

She remained just inside the entrance of her aunt's New England home and watched the departing visitor close the gate to the short picket fence that enclosed their cottage. "That certainly was. . .peculiar," she whispered, unable to voice a more suitable word to describe the unexpected encounter. Never had she known anyone who could make her feel in the span of seconds as if she were both floating above the earth and falling into its depths, an experience most unnerving.

Regardless of his apparent consideration, his furtive manner disturbed her. Charming. Yes, he was that. Attractive. Quietly compelling. But she couldn't fathom how or why his mysterious dark eyes—strangely familiar eyes—had seemed to reach into her soul. That is, if she had anything left of a soul, still tattered and bruised after her most recent quarrel with her aunt, regarding what Aunt Genevieve considered yet another of Angel's faults. She was just glad the dark stranger had gone. He seemed. . .dangerous. That was the word she sought. This day had been difficult enough without adding to its troubles.

Angel firmly closed the door on the stranger and on her thoughts.

"You didn't have to be such a flirt," her cousin Faye reproved bitterly. "I saw how you all but pushed yourself in front of him. Just like you did with Charles."

At the ridiculous accusation, Angel turned to gape at Faye then directed her disbelieving stare toward the foot of the staircase where her other cousin, Rosemary, stood. And glared.

"I answered the door as I always do. With courtesy. The same courtesy I would give to any visitor, whether it's the postman or a member from the women's society or. . .or our most recent guest, who was kind enough to return your parcel."

She wondered why her cousins never extended the same courtesies or acted maturely, for that matter. Though she was younger than Faye by two years, and Rosemary by three, when the stranger rang the bell, returning the package Faye had accidentally dropped on the sidewalk on their way home, Faye acted with all the composure of a silly goose. She had rushed to stand beside Angel and asked the young man a number of meddlesome questions, making Angel wonder if Faye's lost package had been the accident she claimed or a ploy to gain his attention. Rosemary behaved no better, insinuating herself into every sentence when Angel stopped to take a breath in giving the man his requested directions.

In reply to Faye's question about the reason for his visit to their small town, he distantly admitted he came to see a friend. Before Faye could query further, he tipped his hat, expressed relief that he noticed her drop the package, and left. Faye's behavior had been ridiculously childish. She was acting childishly now, and Angel was in no mood to argue about the afternoon's occurrences.

She headed for the stairs.

Rosemary blocked her way.

"You think you're so high and mighty, and the fellas all flock to our door to see you just because some say you're a doll. But that's not enough, is it? You want all the men to notice you. Men like my Charles."

Angel sighed, weary of explaining herself. "I wasn't flirting with Charles at the druggist's, and I certainly wasn't flirting with that stranger. I asked Charles how his mother was since her fall on the ice last winter, and with the man who was just here—well, you heard. He wanted directions to Mayfair Lane, so I gave them to him."

"You did more than that," Faye interrupted. "You smiled at him!"

"I beg your pardon? Since when is smiling considered a crime? I was being polite."

Angel didn't add that the stranger had gotten a more-than-adequate view of Faye's teeth from the many smiles she had directed his way. Such a reminder was petty; besides, it didn't matter what she might say. She had learned long ago that what her cousins considered acceptable for them they regarded as taboo for Angel, no doubt aided by their mother's strong opinions. "For the last time, I have no intention of trying to interest Charles. He isn't my type." Though she wasn't exactly sure what sort of man was.

"Why?" Rosemary's face colored a shade of persimmon as she switched tactics and went to his defense. "You think you're too good for him, is that it? Ha! A lot you know. You're no better than Charles or me or Faye—or anyone in New York for that matter." A cruel smirk lifted her painted red mouth, making her seem like an evil clown. "In fact, you're worse."

"I haven't the time or the desire to continue this conversation." Angel graciously didn't mention that Charles had shown no interest in Rosemary to cause her to become so possessive of him.

She tried to push past, but Rosemary mirrored her action, again blocking her.

"You're such a stickler for the truth? Well, maybe it's high time you had a taste of it, instead of making trouble for others."

Angel sighed. "This is really about what happened the other night, isn't it? I had no idea when your mother came home early and asked where you were that you would be about to cut your hair and she would catch you. You can hardly blame me for what happened."

Her aunt detested the fashionable short bobs for her daughters and had an iron will that Angel's cousins preferred not to cross. Aunt Genevieve didn't care what Angel did. Nor did she bat an eyelash in disapproval when, in an act of self-defiance two years before, Angel cut her easily tangled, waist-length curls into a short, crimped style that stars like Myrna Loy had made popular. Aunt Genevieve even smiled when she noticed the uneven ends of Angel's pathetic attempt.

Rosemary narrowed her eyes. "This is about so much more than Mother taking away my privileges. It has to do with your past. The past you know nothing about."

"Rosemary, don't." Faye's initial malice shifted to abrupt anxiety, as often was the case when she was instantly sorry for her rash words and behavior. "Mama wouldn't like it."

"Mama's not here now, is she? And I think it's time Miss High-and-Mighty was put in her place. What I have to say is the truth. And that's something of which our dear, darling Angel is a strong advocate." She turned cold eyes on Angel. "Isn't that right, Cousin? It's the truth or nothing with you." Her tone gave the pretense of sweetness, while underneath lay something ugly.

"I prefer the truth to a lie." Angel swallowed over the lump of worry clotting her throat. Something odd was going on—her cousins fighting a battle of wills over a hidden disclosure Angel wasn't sure she wanted to hear. "There are also times when it's better to say nothing at all."

"Really?" Rosemary sneered. "Well, too bad for you this isn't one of them. You could have done the same—chosen not to say a word—but you didn't. Now I won't get to dance with Charles at Sharon's party because I won't be able to go!"

Faye stepped forward. "Maybe you should calm down before you say more, Rosemary. You're not thinking clearly."

"On the contrary, I'm thinking very clearly, Faye. I only wish to give our dear, blue-eyed Angel all she deserves and desires—the absolute truth. She's almost eighteen and has a right to know just what a grand lie her life has been."

Disgusted with Rosemary and more than a little nervous about her revelation, Angel turned away. Rosemary grabbed her arm in a grip that made Angel wince. "Oh no, *Cousin dear*. Don't go just yet." Her words came deceitfully sweet. "Wouldn't you like to know the truth of who you are? Of who your mother was—or rather, who she is? Of the freak she turned out to be?"

Faye gasped. "Rosemary, don't!"

"You're lying, as usual." Angel worked to keep her face bland and her voice emotionless, not wanting either of her cousins to see how Rosemary's words tore into her orphaned heart. "My mother is dead. She died when I was three."

"Died? Oh no. Our mother lied to you, Angel. Your mother didn't die, as Mother led you to believe. She gave you to our mother, that much is true. Because she didn't want you. And do you know why?"

Her voice rose in pitch as she stepped closer, her hate-filled eyes burning into Angel's wary ones. Faye grabbed her sister's arm.

"Rosemary, stop it!"

Rosemary shook off her sister's hold, her attention never wavering from Angel.

"She didn't want you with her because she's a sideshow

freak in a traveling carnival. You've heard of the bearded lady, haven't you? Well, if I were you, I'd check the mirror daily, because it might be hereditary. Your mother has a beard thicker than Dr. Meeker's. I know; I've seen pictures. She's nothing but a freak, and she's still very much alive. She sent a letter to Mother two years ago."

"I—I don't believe you." Angel felt her world begin to tilt and grabbed the banister in a white-knuckled grip. Rosemary noticed and bared her teeth in another cruel smile.

"It's true. I saw the letter. Uncle Bruce kept clippings of his years at the carnival. Mother keeps his albums in her room. He worked there as a strong man. He married your mother, likely because he pitied the creature since no other sane man would go near her—she was half a man after all, a *bearded* lady, and who knows what your true father was. Likely some other monstrous freak. You're no relation to our uncle, no relation to anyone in our family—and you know what that means, don't you?"

"Rosemary, that's enough!" Faye's warning shriek hurt Angel's ears. Worry glinted in Faye's eyes as she pulled on her sister's arm with both hands. Rosemary ignored Faye, struggling to remain in place.

"You're nothing but a nameless foundling! Without a true father. With a freak of a mother who never wanted you. You're an illegitimate piece of garbage. A nobody. Hardly normal. And would you like to know the truth of how you came into being?"

Faye jerked Rosemary hard enough to pull her away from Angel and slapped her. Rosemary rubbed her reddened cheek and looked with shock at her sister.

"You know what Mama said would happen if we told. You've said too much already."

Feeling like a witness to a slowly evolving nightmare, Angel watched the usually cowed Faye stand up to her sister.

Rosemary sneered at her. "We're not children anymore. It's time someone set the record straight. Mother should have told her ages ago."

Angel felt as if she'd been sucked into a void; she could scarcely think. Could barely believe what Rosemary said was true. Faye's uncharacteristic behavior seemed to make it all the more horribly real and not some hurtful prank for which Rosemary was known.

"Come upstairs," Rosemary invited with another hateful smirk. "The albums don't lie."

Dread made Angel hold back.

"What?" Rosemary taunted. "Afraid to see the truth with your own eyes? You can spout it about everyone else, but when it's turned around on you, you run away like a coward!"

Angel clamped her lips and straightened her spine, refusing to sink to the stairs in tearful self-pity, as Rosemary no doubt wished. It had been years since she'd shed a tear. She had learned at a young age that crying never helped and often made things worse.

"Very well," she agreed. "Lead the way, Cousin."

Faye eyed Angel with unease while Rosemary regarded her in triumph.

Determined not to bolt, Angel directed her attention to the stairs, trying to ignore her cousins, who might not be cousins at all; they certainly had never treated her as family, though Faye at least seemed to have a conscience. Angel felt surprised her legs could move—they'd begun to tremble so—but she led the sisters to their mother's bedroom. Momentary unease made her hang back on the threshold while they brushed past.

As a child, she'd been forbidden to enter her aunt's personal domain, and not since Rosemary's malicious trick in childhood to lure Angel there and lock her inside to get her in trouble had she ever attempted it. But the sight of the worn leather album her cousin pulled from beneath the bed captured her curiosity. . .and released a wave of foreboding.

Against her better judgment, she moved closer.

Rosemary opened the album's wide pages. A letter fell to the floor. Angel caught the town's name—Coventry—before Faye snatched it up and held it to her breast, as if the envelope contained secret government documents. In the album, newspaper clippings had been pasted on the heavy black pages, along with old photographs.

Rosemary thrust the book under Angel's nose, her index finger pointing to a photograph. "There she is—your mother, Lila! Look and see if you don't believe me. And the brat Uncle Bruce is holding must be you."

With her heart pounding madly, Angel eyed the images, worn and faded from the years. The candid shot showed a group of carnival performers clustered near an erected tent; few acknowledged the camera. The little girl in the bald, heavyset strongman's arms was one of three people posing. Her eyes and smile sparkled as she tilted her head and modeled for whoever held the camera. Surely that couldn't be her! The dark-haired child with the long, tight ringlets seemed much too lighthearted and happy to be Angel.

Stunned, she tore her gaze from the ebullient child and stared at the solemn, dark-haired woman standing at the man's elbow. Young and slender, she wore a veil, Arabian style, hooked across her nose and extending over the lower part of her face. Huge dark eyes, shaped like Angel's, were the only feature clearly seen.

"What is the meaning of this?"

At their mother's forbidding words, Faye scrambled off the bed. Rosemary dropped the book. Numb from so many revelations in so short a time, Angel didn't jump in guilty shock like the others, didn't do anything but blink and stare.

A scowl darkened Aunt Genevieve's features. Her gaze dropped to the open album on the floor. Immediately her snapping dark eyes lifted and ensnared Angel's.

"M—mother," Rosemary gasped, "we didn't expect you back so soon."

"The meeting ended early." Her eyes glittered. "Girls, go to your room. I'll deal with you later."

Angel snapped out of her trance and moved after them, also hoping for escape.

"Angelica, you will remain. I must speak with you."

With a heart that furiously pounded and sank deeper each moment that passed, Angel stood, rooted, and awaited her fate.

⁂

Five long hours later, when all was dark and the occupants of the house lay sleeping, Angel tiptoed downstairs, clutching a train case and one bigger satchel—all she could carry with all she owned in the world. In the larger case rested her uncle's album, which her aunt practically shoved at her when Angel quietly asked if she might look at it. She felt no remorse in taking the album, one of three, since it contained only clippings of her mother and husband and their life at the carnival. As much as she hated Angel's mother, Aunt Genevieve would have no wish to keep the memento and likely had forgotten she owned it.

All that Rosemary said was true; Aunt Genevieve verified it in cutting, concise words. Equally distressing, her aunt informed Angel that she owed it to her to marry the man of her choosing, and her aunt's choice made Angel shiver with revulsion: Benjamin Crane, one of the meanest, oldest, and richest misers in all of Lanville, who'd often leered at Angel. According to her aunt, Angel, being nameless, would never make a better match or find another man who'd want her, and Angel should consider it an honor to be presented with such an "auspicious opportunity." Auspicious for her aunt, maybe, but not for Angel. Her aunt went on to say that the

Depression had hit all of them hard, but she'd provided for Angel, who should consider herself fortunate not to have been kicked out on the street to fend for herself.

Except for her companionship with the friendly cook, Nettie, Angel almost wished her aunt had kicked her out. She certainly wouldn't marry Mr. Crane, old enough to be her grandfather, and felt a bit like Cinderella escaping her evil stepmother and wicked stepsisters. But no glass slippers existed for her, no magical ball to attend, and certainly no prince. Only the distant memory of a forgotten mother urged her down the silent road, along with the faintest recollection of her sweet scent and the gentle wisps of a song, perhaps an old lullaby, crooned in a voice that soothed Angel. The fleeting memory visited her both awake and asleep, and Angel reasoned any woman with such a voice couldn't be the vindictive monster her aunt described.

She wasn't sure how she felt to have a mother people thought of as a traveling carnival oddity, but above all else, she wished to find her. Even the ambiguity of her quest was preferable to the certainty of her future if she stayed in Lanville. Perhaps she might learn what it felt like to be happy like the little girl in the picture.

Her emotions dictated every action; reason had long fled. She refused to think beyond the flicker of hope that her mother might want to know her, that somehow her absence had all been a dreadful mistake.

The streets remained eerily quiet; not even a dog barked. Angel kept close to the elm trees, should the need to duck behind one for cover present itself. The neighbors thought highly of her aunt, who involved herself in charitable endeavors, and would no doubt report Angel's whereabouts should they peek through their curtains and see her skulking in the night with her luggage.

The windows of the houses remained dark, quiet. Yet

her heart raced with each sudden snap and creak, sure she would soon be caught.

How much time elapsed before she reached the train depot, Angel didn't know. Her feet in her pumps hurt dreadfully, her legs, almost-numb, throbbed, and her stockings did little to keep out the chill night air. A late March wind blew sharp and cold beneath her calf-length skirt, and she pulled her coat closer beneath her chin as she approached the ticket window and took a place in line.

"A one-way ticket to Coventry, Connecticut, please," she informed the bespectacled man when her turn came, mentioning the town she'd seen on the envelope before Faye grabbed it.

"Certainly, miss. That'll be three dollars."

"So much?" she asked, her hopes plummeting. "I'm only going one way."

"That'll still be three dollars."

"Thank you, but. . .I—I've changed my mind."

Crestfallen, she moved away. The next gentleman in line quickly stepped up and took her place at the window before the idea surfaced to ask the stationmaster where two dollars and twenty-five cents would take her. Eyeing the line that had grown by half, Angel decided to continue down the platform. She should have taken a bus. She'd had no idea traveling by train would cost more than she possessed, the last of her earnings from working at the soda fountain before Mr. Hanson needed to dismiss her, unable to continue paying her wages. To her knowledge, which tonight had proven sadly deficient, she'd never taken a train; according to the picture in the album, she had. The photograph showed she had actually lived on one.

Too weary to walk even half a block more, she mulled over what to do. She couldn't return to her aunt's home and be forced to marry Benjamin Crane. Angel's life would then be over. . . .

The shrill call of a train whistle captured her absorbed attention. Without really giving the linked cars conscious thought, she stared at the long line of them on the nearest track.

"Mommy," she heard a little boy ask the woman holding his hand. "Is Coventry very far? How long till we get there? Will we be there soon?"

"Yes, Coventry is very far, Timmy, and we will get there when we get there. Hush now."

Angel watched mother and son move up the metal stairs of the car nearest her. A porter took their bulky case, helping the heavyset woman into the confined area. He looked toward Angel for a fearful heartbeat, and she wondered if he could read her mind. His eyes narrowed suspiciously. Her face went warm.

Quickly she averted her gaze down the length of the platform, pretending to look for someone. After a moment she allowed her attention to return and noted with relief the trio had disappeared inside the train. Through a line of filthy windows, Angel watched their progress down the aisle.

The train began to move. Each entrance glided past. Her heart began to race.

Did she dare?

An image of Nettie's disapproving features filled Angel's mind, but she was desperate. And besides, she didn't have that far to go.

Before the train trundled past, Angel threw her largest case up into one of the last entrances—grateful fate was at least kind enough that the case didn't rebound and spill onto the platform. Running to catch up, she barely jumped aboard herself, using one hand to grab the rail.

She made it!

She took a deep, shaky breath. Once she regained her equilibrium and her satchel, she approached the railcar on her right, wishing to get as far as possible from the shrewd porter and find somewhere to hide.

The door flew inward beneath her grip.

She inhaled a startled gasp as both the experience and the abrupt motion of the train's increasing speed made her stumble forward. A man's strong hand grabbed her arm to steady her, and for the second time that day, she dazedly blinked up into the enigmatic eyes of the tall, dark stranger who'd visited her aunt's home.

two

Roland stared into a pair of bewitching eyes, as dark a blue gray as the Atlantic at dusk. It took him a moment to realize where he'd seen such eyes, and the jolt made him go stock-still.

"You," he said at the same moment her lips silently formed the word.

A brown hat was smashed down over thick, shoulder-length hair the color of sable, curly wisps blew into her face, and the ruffled edge of a scarf wrapped around her neck covered much of her jawline. But he couldn't mistake those rich, deep eyes.

"Did you follow me?" he asked in puzzled amusement. He assumed she hoped for either the opportunity of a handout or the prospect of a good time.

"F–follow you?" she spluttered. "Of course not! I wouldn't dream of doing such a thing."

"No need to go berserk. It was only a question."

The dame's icy courtesy and frosty smiles from that afternoon should have been enough to give him an account of her feelings for his company. She frowned, clearly unhappy to see him again. The cold air from the train in motion whipped through the opening between railcars. With his hand still closed around her arm, he pulled her inside and slammed the door shut behind them.

His intention of securing a newspaper no longer important, Roland turned to his unexpected guest. With a quick appraisal, he noted her tousled, windblown appearance and breathless manner, as if she'd run a long distance to make it to the train on time. Two spots of red colored high cheekbones belonging to

18

a flawless face—what he could see of it—and she gripped the luggage handles in tight, gloved fists. A real doll, chinalike in appearance. But a hint of panic made her wide eyes even bigger, her full lips drawn and tense, and he wondered if she might lash out at him with her bags if he were to take a step closer.

He decided not to take the risk.

"The bends in the track can knock you off your feet. I'd advise you take a seat, Miss. . . ?"

Ignoring his hint to learn her name, she looked around, her manner distantly assured, as if she had every right to be there and he was the intruder. Her brow wrinkled in confusion when she saw the small drawing room, containing dual leather benches with high backs, the length of twin settees. She moved to one and set her bags down with a muffled thump. Without a word, she sank to the padded seat nearest the dual windows and pulled away her scarf.

Curious about his new cabinmate, he took the seat opposite, farthest from where she sat and closest to the door. If not for the fact that she gave him directions earlier, he might think her mute. Minute after taut minute stretched in silence.

"Something of a coincidence, bumping into you like this." He tried to initiate conversation, hoping it wouldn't crackle with tension like the quiet between them did.

"Yes." Her expression guarded, she afforded him the barest glance and pulled the fingers of each glove, one by one, removing the peeling leather. They, like the rest of her outerwear, appeared years old. With the nation in crisis, few had the luxury of buying a new winter coat, except for Roland, who could buy the train on which they sat if he wished, paid for with the dirty simoleons earned in others' blood.

He grimaced at the thought.

Her gaze remained fixed to the spotted window and the trees and buildings that hurried past in a dark, watercolor blur.

"Two strangers meeting twice in one day in the oddest of

circumstances and on opposite sides of town—that's one for the books, isn't it? And now, here we are, sharing a car on the same train." He smiled. She didn't return the favor, behaving in a way similar to what she'd done at the house. Was it just him, or did all men provoke this sort of reaction?

She pulled a handkerchief from her handbag, put it to her nose, and sniffled. She didn't appear to be crying; her eyes were dry.

"Did you catch a chill?"

She shrugged one shoulder and looked back through the window.

"It's nasty weather to be out. I don't know about you, but I've had enough of this blustery cold and rain. I suppose we should be thankful it didn't rain today."

She gave him the barest inclination of her head in agreement.

"Are you visiting family in Connecticut?"

Her eyes cut to him, shocked, cautious. "Yes. Family." She sniffled again into her handkerchief. "Please, if you don't mind, I believe I have caught a chill. I really don't feel up to small talk."

"I can ask the steward to fetch you a hot toddy—"

"No." He barely got the suggestion out before she cut him off. "Thank you." Her words tried to be polite. She fidgeted in a clear attempt to get comfortable in her seat. "I'm fine."

Observing her clear distress, Roland doubted that but didn't insist. He grew silent and wished now he'd gotten that newspaper. Spoiled when it came to a social life, as the minutes ticked by with the clacking of train wheels marking each second, he felt restless. His aloof cabinmate had closed her eyes. Judging by the anxious frown wrinkling the pale skin between her eyebrows, he didn't think she was sleeping.

The door to the car swung open, and a Pullman porter appeared.

"Sorry, sir." He nodded to Roland.

The woman's eyes flew open. Dread inscribed her every feature as the dark-skinned man turned his attention on her and approached like a persistent fox cornering a frightened rabbit. With swift understanding Roland recognized the problem.

The porter looked between Roland and the woman, clearly noting the taut distance between them. "May I see your ticket, miss?" He held out his hand, palm up, a grim look entering his attentive eyes.

"My ticket?" Her words came raspy.

"Yes'm. Your ticket. The one you bought to board this train."

"I. . ." She pushed her shoulders into the seat, cowering within herself, the motion almost undetectable except that Roland intently watched her. "I'm afraid I didn't, th–that is I don't–"

"The lady's with me." He captured their startled attention.

"With you, sir?" The man's attitude jumped a notch higher to deferential respect.

"I trust that's not a problem?"

"No, sir. Not at all." The porter literally backed up to the door. If Roland weren't so disgusted by his name and all it accomplished, he might have found the entire situation bizarrely amusing. "Sorry for the misunderstanding. Didn't realize you were traveling with a guest, sir."

Roland magnanimously waved him off, though his smile felt tight. "Don't concern yourself. I didn't mention it when I boarded."

"If there's anything I can get you, sir?"

"A newspaper would be nice."

"Yes, sir. Would a copy of the *New York Times* be all right, sir?"

"That's fine." He kept his voice pleasant. "And next time, if you would be kind enough to knock first rather than barge inside and scare the living daylights out of the lady, I'd appreciate it."

The steward's eyes grew larger. "Yes, sir. I—I only thought . . . . Yes, sir, of course, sir." He wiped his brow with a handkerchief, backed out, and shut the door.

Roland turned his attention to the woman. He leaned forward in friendly persuasion, keen for a little conversation. "Maybe now that that little matter has been taken care of, you'd care to relax, miss, and we can get to know one another better?" He hoped for a smile at the least. At the most, words of thanks and a thaw of her chilly personality.

At least she was no longer coldly distant.

Her smoky eyes sparked with a fire in danger of incinerating him. Resentment stiffened her shoulders, and he wondered what he'd said or done this time to earn such an unfavorable reaction.

"Thank you for taking care of 'that little matter,' " she said with lips pulled tight, sounding more as if she were telling him to get lost, "though I didn't ask for your help. And just so we're clear, I'm not some damsel in distress looking for a wandering knight to rush in and rescue me. I'll certainly never let you lure me into becoming your. . .your"—intense color heightened her cheeks—"your floozy!"

Entirely baffled by her response, he watched as in hot indignation she stood up, grabbed her bags, and whisked from his compartment.

❧

Angel had no idea of where she was headed. She only knew she must get away from the insufferable Casanova in the car behind her. Had she stayed, she might have blurted something she would dearly regret.

Juggling her cases to open the door, she went into the next car, finding it to be a sleeping car with curtains covering the berths. She quietly went through another, hearing snores, then another. As she moved through to the next car, she wondered if he tried to make moves on all lone female travelers or if she'd been his only hapless victim.

An attractive face didn't always go hand in hand with a pleasant disposition—a morsel of wisdom she'd learned while observing some of the dapper young fellows who visited the soda fountain. A good thing, too, that she knew better than to be captivated by his suave charisma and dashing smile. She understood the foolish danger of allowing herself to be taken in by such a rogue. In that single regard her aunt had not failed her, stressing to Angel that once the truth of her birthright surfaced no decent man would have her. And she didn't want a man who wasn't decent. She may have been conceived in sin and loathing, as Aunt Genevieve almost gleefully informed her, but she wouldn't succumb to a sordid life because of what had happened to her mother or the choices she had made, most of which Angel still didn't know in full or even if they were true.

The porter suddenly moved through the opposite door, *his* newspaper in hand. She tensed as the man noticed the luggage she carried. Rather than call her bluff, he offered a courteous if cool smile. "Is there a problem, miss?"

Still leery of him, she didn't answer right away. At least he didn't ask to see her ticket again, and she felt a niggling sense of guilt that she didn't have one.

He studied her as if she didn't belong there.

She swallowed hard. "Where can I buy a cup of coffee?"

His gaze again darted to her luggage, his eyes curious as they lifted to hers. "You'll be wanting the dining car, miss. Follow me." Before she could protest that she could find the car alone with his directions, he turned and walked back the way he had come. With no choice but to follow, she did, hoping she wasn't walking into a trap.

They reached the car, and he spoke to another man, a

steward in a different white uniform. Instead of benches, small tables covered in white cloths lined both sides. She headed down the narrow aisle toward one then heard the steward clear his throat. When she looked, he shook his head for her to stop.

Her heart pounded. Had she been caught?

The porter left, and the steward motioned she should leave her luggage to the side, by the door. With such restricted space, she had little choice. He led her to a different table from what she would have chosen—far in the back, this one finer. A thin silver vase with a pink rose decorated its center.

She glanced at her first choice toward the front of the car and closer to her luggage. "I think I would prefer a table in the front—"

"I was told to seat you here." The man stood ramrod straight, unrelenting, his blue eyes refusing resistance. He held out a chair. Uneasy, she slid into it, feeling closed in as he scooted her closer. She shook off the crazy notion; the train encounter with the rogue stranger had definitely rattled her trust.

A black waiter soon appeared. After convincing him she wanted only coffee, knowing she must be stingy with her meager funds, he left. She took the peaceful opportunity to watch the few diners and figured it must be near closing time. Did the dining car close? A businessman sat alone, reading his newspaper. An elderly couple shared a meal. Two women with similar features, likely mother and daughter, chatted across a table in friendly conversation. Angel found herself studying them in wistful reflection, wondering if she might one day have as comfortable a relationship with her mother. . .if she could find her.

Engrossed in observing the two women, she took little notice that another passenger had entered the dining car. Not until the steward brought the newcomer to her table did she look up, dismayed to see the stranger. The third time to meet him by happenstance.

Wry amusement lit his dark eyes, but before she could protest to him about sharing her table, the steward moved away, almost bowing and scraping as he promised the man his "usual." The porter had also behaved like a serf eager to please the lord of the castle. Clearly the staff knew him well, and he was a man of means, accustomed to having his wishes obeyed.

Her observation brought back the feeling of being cornered.

"Well, well, what do you know?" He took the chair across from her, apparently unaware of her mounting apprehension. "We meet again. This is a surprise."

Angel noted the many empty tables he could have chosen. "Is it?"

He narrowed his eyes cautiously. "I'm not sure I get your meaning."

"You accused me of following you. But maybe the shoe is on the other foot and you're the one following me." She tried to come across as cool and collected. "I'm afraid I might have given you the wrong impression. I'm not interested in any sort of. . .alliance. I'm not the sort of girl to engage in. . .casual acquaintances." Her face burned with embarrassment as she tried to express her standards in a delicate manner.

He lifted his hand to stop her. "Before you pursue that thought, miss, honest, all I came here for was a ham on rye and club soda."

"And you chose my table as the spot to eat your meal?" she scoffed with a little huff of breath. "It's one thing that we coincidentally found ourselves in the same car, but you purposely chose to sit here."

"Your table?" That irritating glint of amusement again danced in his eyes. "Then you really don't know. . . ."

"What should I know?" A mounting sense of dread made her slightly ill.

He settled back in his chair. "I've been remiss. We were never introduced, and I'm afraid there's been a misunderstanding."

"Oh, really?" She thought she'd read him well. Even now he studied her features from face to form, as far as the table edge allowed, as if he liked what he saw. She squirmed, her aunt's chilling words weighing on her mind. "When you said you wanted to get to know me better. . ."

"I meant just that. Getting to know you in what I hoped would be friendlier conversation than we've had so far. Nothing more. You might find this difficult to believe, but I'm not the sort to take advantage of casual acquaintances either."

He looked and sounded sincere, his dark eyes undemanding, his deep voice gentle. She relaxed a fraction, allowing him a small smile. Maybe she was overreacting; this evening had been traumatic. "I'll admit, my first impression of you was of a wealthy playboy or gigolo who makes the round of New York's finest speakeasies twice a weekend and lives on a diet of dry martinis and gin."

He fidgeted, glancing away. She guessed she'd hit the mark on one item, perhaps all of them.

"I take it dry martinis are your poison of preference?" he asked in a sociable manner.

"I don't drink. My aunt's a teetotaler—there's never been a drop of liquor in the cabinets. Even cooking sherry. And except for sipping a glass of white wine and finding it awfully bitter, I've never tasted alcohol. I mentioned gin and dry martinis because that seems to be what all the wealthy, disreputable playboys drink. Like Nick Charles."

"Ah." He smiled. "Good ole Nick. So, you're a gumshoe buff. I take it you've seen *The Thin Man?*"

"Since I lost my job, thanks to the economy, I don't go to the theater anymore. I like to read, and Dashiell Hammett wrote the mystery as a book before it became a motion picture, you know," she teased.

She couldn't believe how easily they were conversing, when minutes ago she'd done all she could to dodge his questions, to dodge him. He had a way about him, a strange charisma that made her relax while at the same time her pulse raced. She hadn't thought it possible to feel both calm and breathless at once.

"Is that what led you to travel?" he asked with that same quiet that invited a confidence. "Are you hoping to find work in another city?"

Angel blinked, surprised he so aptly read her dilemma. "Something like that."

"What I don't understand is why you would leave your family to look for work in another state. Are things that bad at home?"

Seeing the kindness in his eyes, she didn't take offense at his question.

"Let's just say I realized it was time I left my aunt's charity and found a way to make a living."

"So you took off in the night and stowed aboard a train. Don't worry," he quietly assured. "I won't tell a soul. Why do you think I spoke up for you?"

She glanced around nervously. "Why did you? I wasn't exactly nice." She drew her brows together in concern. "Is it so obvious? I mean—*what I did*?" She mouthed the last three words.

He studied her until a flush warmed her face. "The porter isn't going to care one way or the other as long as the fare is covered. Don't worry about that. As to why, let's just say I felt the urge to. . .help a damsel in distress." He grinned.

At the memory of her parting shot, she lowered her eyes and shook her head in embarrassment.

"Though I'm not sure anyone who knows me would call me a knight. Maybe a black knight. . ."

At his wry, amused response, she swiftly raised her head.

"No, don't look at me like that. Your virtue is safe. I have no intention of 'luring you to become my floozy,' I believe is how you put it?"

Rather than be insulted or injured by his light tone that gently teased, she found herself nervously laughing.

"I was a bit high-strung, but can you blame me? You pulled me into the car, one that had no other passengers, asked a lot of personal questions, told the steward to knock first, then told me you wanted to get to know me better. What's a girl supposed to think?"

He chuckled, a dimple she'd never noticed flashing in his cheek. "Okay, maybe I was overfriendly. But I couldn't get over the shock of running into you again in another strange twist of fate. It seemed. . .uncanny."

She nodded, deciding to trust him with part of her dilemma since he'd guessed the truth about the rest and hadn't turned her over to the authorities. "I've never done anything like this before. Sneaking aboard, I mean. I've never taken one red cent or even a stick of candy as a child. But tonight I acted before I thought."

"I believe you."

She studied him in confusion, having been sure she would need to persuade him. "Why? You don't know me."

"Let's just say I have a hunch you're the type of dame who'd never resort to such measures unless you were desperate. Again, don't worry about them finding out." He casually directed a thumb over his shoulder as he spoke. "Your secret's safe with me."

"I'll pay you back, of course." She didn't like being indebted to anyone, especially not this man whose name she still didn't know. "Give me an address where I should send the money, and I'll reimburse you as soon as I find work."

"There's no need. It was nothing. I have plenty." He grimaced, as if being wealthy actually displeased him.

"I insist." She vainly searched through her purse. Feeling silly, she looked up. "It seems I'll need to borrow a pen and something to write on, too."

He eyed her a long moment. She wished she knew what was running through his mind.

"Tell you what. Let's forget all about that, and let me try introducing myself again. We got off track the first time. Hopefully the conductor isn't as lousy at steering this train as I am at managing a conversation."

She smiled at his little joke.

"I'm Roland."

"Angel." He lifted his brows at her reply, and she added, "My name. A nickname I've grown used to. My full name is Angelica Mornay."

"It suits you. Pretty name for a pretty dame."

His casual compliment left her ill at ease, and she looked down, snapping her purse shut.

"Did I say something wrong?"

Before she could respond, the waiter returned to the table with their orders. "If there will be anything else, Mr. Piccoli, please do not hesitate to ask."

"Bring the lady a sandwich as well. I'm sure she must be hungry."

The shock of hearing his name struck Angel like an unexpected dousing of icy water; she couldn't think to respond or refuse. A kaleidoscope of startling facts twisted inside her mind, making her dizzy.

Roland Piccoli! Grandson of the notorious gangster Vittorio Piccoli. . .who dispensed with his enemies as casually as she dispensed with a pair of damaged stockings. No wonder he seemed familiar when she saw him at her aunt's! His face had been plastered in the society pages a month ago, a blushing debutante on his arm, who the article had said was his fiancée. And Angel had run across his path, not once but twice. . . .

Walking twice into the path of a killer.

He seemed not to notice her horror as he spoke with the waiter.

The curiosity she had shoved aside earlier raced to the forefront of her memory in a blaze of enlightenment: the cars, all of them crowded, full of smoke. The car she shared with him, empty of passengers, no smoke. Even decorated, she realized now, and differently than the others! She didn't know much about trains or fares or the cars in which passengers rode, but with sudden and certain knowledge, she knew she'd found her way into his private car.

Of all the foolish, dangerous moves she could make, this was the worst!

The Piccoli family owned gambling houses and night-clubs in all of New York City. At the soda fountain, she occasionally overheard the men she served talk with each other in awed, fear-filled conversation about the Piccolis' latest manner of doing "business" or "collecting" a debt. Those owing money suddenly disappeared or were found washed up by the river.

She couldn't imagine that this grandson of one of the worst crime bosses in the Big Apple, seated across from her and now staring at her with narrowed eyes, would lower himself to sit in a crowded, public dining car. The steward and all his entourage would probably fall over themselves in their readiness to please him by serving him dinner in his private car.

So why was he here?

The answer was obvious.

And now she, too, owed him a debt.

The car felt suddenly close, smothering her, and she desperately sucked in air. Hurriedly she stood, knocking into the table and spilling her coffee on the pristine cloth. Her chair almost flew backward, hitting the wall. The thought of the lifeblood his family just as easily spilled with horrifying regularity and without remorse made her scramble a step backward in retreat. Perhaps it wasn't her blood he would seek in payment for the favor of his silence, if she should refuse his wishes, or even her money as the reimbursement. But it didn't take her two guesses to figure out what he did want, despite his claim to the contrary. His gentle, sympathetic manner was all a seduction; once again in her life she'd been easy to deceive.

"Angel, what's wrong?"

"Nothing." Except that her voice sounded too high-pitched to convince him of that. "I. . .need to find the lavatory."

"I can't help you. I don't leave my family's private car often." Of course he didn't.

"But I felt like company tonight and decided to eat at my table. Little did I know I'd entertain such charming company."

His table. Of course! Now she understood his earlier words.

Managing a flip response, though she had no idea what she said, she pretended nonchalance and walked away from his table, toward her luggage, toward the exit, toward freedom. . . .

She wanted to scream bloody murder and run.

three

Angel darted a look over her shoulder. The immediate threat to her life still sat with his back to her. She grabbed her luggage and hurried out. At last, finding the lavatory, she managed to get both herself and the luggage inside the cramped area. She doused her face with water, trying to steady her nerves. Her fingers trembled as she let the cold liquid run through them, then patted her cheeks and turned off the faucet.

Of all the dumb luck. To find herself sharing a car and a table opposite a man with a family as dangerous as Al Capone. Not sharing a car. Sharing his car. His private car. And his table!

But what else could she expect? She had broken the law in stowing aboard, and Nettie's warning words of "*those who do evil, reap evil*" reverberated in her mind. She had entered the world of crime tonight; was it any wonder the first man to greet her would be a criminal?

If she believed in a God who cared, she would go to Him and plead for help out of this mess. Too long Angel had walked alone, learning from childhood that no one cared, except maybe one. "Nettie," she whispered, looking into the mirror, "I wish you were here with your wise advice." Her friend would probably quote scripture, but that usually comforted Angel rather than made her angry.

Once again the solution was up to her. And she had to think of something fast. She couldn't hole herself away forever.

Shutting her eyes to her pale image, she groaned. She must keep her distance, allow no more unforeseen meetings. But how? With little room to hide, if he pursued her, he would find her. He had the entire staff at his beck and call, whereas she had no one to give her aid.

A swift knock made her heart give a painful jump. *Relax, Angel, it's a public room after all.*

Breathing in deeply, she exited. The mother and child she'd seen on the platform stood in the corridor. The woman eyed Angel toting her luggage with a curious nod. The boy tugged on his mother's coat.

"Please, Mama. I wanna go to the cawnival. Can't we go to Grampa's later?"

"We can go to your grandfather's now, and if you're very good, perhaps I'll take you to the carnival when we return," the obviously harried mother replied.

"But what if it's not there anymore?"

"Hush, Timmy, and be a good boy. If we don't visit your grandfather first, we'll not have one thin dime to do anything."

"Will Grampa give us a dime?"

His mother smiled sadly. "I hope he'll give us more than that." She smiled at Angel, almost apologetically. "Would you mind keeping an eye on him?"

"I. . ." Angel swallowed, glancing at the boy and then in the direction of the dining car, several cars away.

"I won't be but a moment," the woman assured.

Angel nodded.

Once the woman closed the door behind her, Angel offered the child an uncertain smile. "Your name is Timmy?" He looked about four.

He nodded in an exaggerated motion, his big brown eyes wide under his tweed cap.

"Did you say something about a carnival, Timmy?"

Again he nodded, and her pasted smile grew genuine. He was such a sweet thing.

"The man said it's at the next stop." He pointed to the front of the train.

"Really? How fortunate. . ."

He cocked his head, wrinkling his nose in confusion. "Huh?"

She chuckled and tweaked his cap. "A grown-up word. It means that hope might just be around the corner."

He grinned. "You're pretty."

His adoring words made her a little sad. "Oh, Timmy. Pretty is nice, but it can bring a world of trouble. It's not so important how one looks, and trust me, pretty is a lot more pain than it's worth."

Again he looked at her strangely. She shook her head with a cheerless smile, realizing a boy his age wouldn't understand even if she did try to explain, so she offered a soft "Thank you" instead. It had taken a lifetime of informative and often painful experience to acknowledge what she had told Timmy. Only a person's character and heart made them beautiful, like Nettie, who was plain with buck teeth but possessed a warm heart and caring disposition that made her beautiful to Angel. Not for the first time since she'd been told of her existence, Angel wondered what type of heart her mother had.

It seemed that for once in her life, Fate or Providence or maybe even Nettie's God had offered a way of escape. And she might find the answers she so desperately craved.

The woman returned, and Angel continued on, finding herself in a coach car with benches on each side. She looked for a place to sit, feeling like a forlorn sparrow teetering on the edge of a cramped nest of sleek ravens. All these people, many of whom appeared to be businessmen in three-piece dark suits, knew exactly who they were and where they were headed. They each wore a confident look of self-assurance that their travels would take them where they wanted to be. She knew where she wanted to go but wasn't sure where her journey would end or what awaited her. A strange thought to flit through her mind while standing in an impossibly narrow aisle amid passengers seated in detached boredom. She found an empty aisle spot next to a gentleman who lay with his head back, his hat tipped over his face.

Now if the train would only get to the next stop before Deadly Enemy Number One went on the prowl and hunted her down.

❧

"More coffee, Mr. Piccoli?"

"Excuse me?" Roland snapped from his musings. "Oh, coffee. No thanks." Before the waiter could leave, he added, "The lady who was with me. Have you seen her?"

"Not for some time, sir. She took her luggage, so my guess is she's getting off at the next stop." He glanced out the window as the train slowed. "Which we're coming to now."

Roland tried to process the information that Angel had taken her luggage with her to the lavatory.

"If there's nothing else, sir?"

"No, nothing. Thank you." Once the waiter left, Roland turned his attention to the window, deep in thought. The muted light from a lamppost flooded the station platform coming into view.

He'd felt drawn to Angel since she opened the door of the cottage and he witnessed her commendable patience with her family members as she attempted several times to give him directions. Here on the train, he had witnessed her fire and spirit but something more, something hidden surfacing for moments at a time. She retained a simple childlike innocence, no matter how daring she might appear. A girl, barely a woman, who would stow away in the night to escape. . .what?

She had been stunned and unnerved to learn his identity. He was accustomed to such a reaction, and he couldn't blame her for leaving his company. His family had amassed the worst of reputations. But still he wondered what had brought her to flee to this train in the first place, and he hoped for a second chance to ask.

The locomotive's short whistle pierced his thoughts. The train slowed and stopped. Passengers disembarked. A familiar navy coat and brown hat caught his eye, the colors faded in the weak light of the station's yellow bulb but leaving no doubt of who they belonged to. She darted a furtive glance over her shoulder, as if uncertain where to go. Roland doubted anyone was coming to meet her, doubted, in fact, that Danbury was her stop.

As he watched, she approached a porter and spoke with him. He pointed to his right, and she turned to look. Roland also looked, seeing nothing but unlit buildings leading to a dark road fringed with dense trees. Through them, hundreds of incandescent lights flickered in the distance, but no buildings stood in sight. She nodded, picked up her luggage, and moved in that direction. His attention suddenly fixed upon three boys, up to no good from the looks of them, who detached themselves from the station's brick wall where they'd been casually leaning.

Roland jumped to his feet as the boys moved to follow Angel.

≈

Angel slowed her nervous pace, not wishing to turn her ankle on loose pebbles that made up the lane traveling into the distance, farther than she could see in the dark. At some point it then twisted to the right and led to a lit-up fairground. To her immediate right, through a gap in the trees, a field offered a shortcut to get there in half the time, without fences or other obstacles to bar her way. Hoping no snakes or mice inhabited the area or, at the very least, were in a deep sleep far beneath the earth, she chose the shortest route.

Her heels partially sank in the soil but not so badly she couldn't manage the walk. Halfway across, a rustling disturbed the grasses behind her. Worried that she had aroused some small nocturnal creature, she swung around in defense, clutching her luggage handles hard.

No vicious animal posed a threat, but three boys, the oldest at least three years her junior but almost as tall, closed in on her. The carnival lights lit up the taunting leers that marred their young faces.

"What do you want?" She backed up.

"The dame's a looker, boys, but dumb as dirt," the tall one said. "Whadda ya think we want, lady? Hand over your money and your jewelry."

Dazed, she gaped at them, unable to grasp what they wanted.

"Well? Whatcha waitin' for? Christmas?" he sneered.

"I—I haven't got much. Two dollars and spare change." At his menacing stare, she opened her purse and pulled out the bills. "See? B–b–but you can have it all. Here." She offered it to them with a shaking hand. "Just p–please. Go away."

He snatched up the money. "What about your jewelry?"

"I don't own any jewelry."

"All dames got some kinda jewels on 'em, 'specially those out so late at night. You want that we should show we're serious?" He threw a sidelong glance to his two cohorts. "Come on, boys. Let's show her how serious we can be."

They moved forward as a group.

"Leave me alone!" Frantic, she swung her heaviest case in a sideways arc, the momentum compromising her balance. She barely managed not to fall. The hoodlums jumped a step back and spread out, stalking her a second time. She swung both pieces of luggage, swinging herself around, gratified when she heard a smack as one case hit the nearest ruffian.

"Now you asked for it," he muttered, rubbing his bruised arm.

"I don't think so." A menacing baritone cut through the night.

Angel looked with shock behind her. She had been so intent on defending herself she hadn't heard his approach.

"Give the lady back her dough, and you boys beat it."

"Yeah? Who's gonna make me? You?" The leader of the bullies swung around in defiance. The boy's hand moved to his pocket. He pulled out a switchblade. "Maybe me and my pals here don't wanna go till we're good and ready. So who says we have to?"

Roland stood his ground, not looking the least bit daunted by the wicked blade that gleamed in the carnival lights. "I say."

"And just who are you, givin' out orders like you own the world? The president? The pope?" The lead hooligan snickered, and the other two joined him.

Roland's answering smile was grim. "Name's Piccoli. Roland Piccoli." He paused for effect. The boys darted anxious glances at one another. "I'm not an important leader, like those you mentioned. But my family eats runts like you for breakfast."

"H–h–how do we know you're not lyin' and are really one of the Piccoli mob?" the first boy stammered, though he tried to appear brave. "Them gangsters do their business in New York City."

"It's him, Johnny," one of the boys argued nervously. "I seen his picture in the newspaper. It's him, I tell ya!"

"Yes, it's me." Roland's words were quiet and sinister, like a loaded gun aimed in their direction. "So I suggest you boys take my advice and scram. I don't ever want to see your faces again."

"No harm done, mister. We wasn't gonna hurt her none." The leader threw the money at Roland's feet then looked at his friends. "Let's get outta here."

With mixed feelings, Angel watched the boys take off running. She worried she might now be in a more precarious situation, alone with a true gangster, and wondered if he carried a gun. She doubted a switchblade would be his weapon of choice. Warily she watched him pick up the money and turn his attention on her, the first time he'd looked at her since his stealthy arrival.

"I—I have to be going," she said quickly. "Thanks for stepping in once again. Good-bye."

She turned but should have known he wouldn't let her get away so easily.

"Don't you want your money?"

She hesitated and moved to take it, but he continued holding it.

"What do you think you're doing out here in the middle of nowhere?" Annoyance put a sharp bite to his words. "Are you screwy or a complete dingbat?"

"My reasons don't concern you."

"Maybe not. But surely you've got more brains in that doll-like head than to walk alone in an empty field at night. In a place you don't even know!"

The reminder that his entire family were notorious criminals faded in the rise of her irritation.

"It's really none of your business." She walked away from him.

His steps followed. "I'm making it my business. If I hadn't come along when I did, those gangster pretenders could have robbed you, or worse."

"I was handling the situation."

He snorted in cynical amusement. "Oh really? How? By boxing with your luggage?"

She whirled to face him and stumbled on uneven ground. He grabbed her arms, letting go the moment she was steady.

"You can hardly keep yourself upright in those crazy things." With disdain he regarded her inadequate pumps. "This is nuts. You're nuts. Why'd you run from the safety of the train into the dark of night and nowhere? My guess is

Danbury wasn't your original stop."

"Again, not your business, Mr. Piccoli," she seethed between her teeth. "I'm managing just fine."

"No you're not, and if you'd stop behaving like an ungrateful brat and take a good look around while you reflect on the past few minutes, you'd realize it, too." His voice gentled. "Look, I'm not the threat here." He reached for her case, taking it before she could argue, and stuffed the bills in her hand. "They're scared off for now, but I don't trust those boys to keep their distance. Let's return to the road. With any luck, a car will drive by and we won't have to walk all the way to the station. I promise I'll leave you alone if you'll just get back on a train and out of harm's way."

"I'm not going back." She tried and failed to retrieve her case, blowing out a frustrated breath at his persistence. "I'm . . .looking for work. Like I told you."

"Where?" He dryly scanned the vast area. "As a tiller of the field? Were you going to ask the squirrels to hire you?"

"Funny man." She glared at him. "In case it's missed your notice, there's a carnival over there."

"Yeah, so?" He regarded her in stunned disbelief. "You're hoping to find work at the *carnival*? Wait a minute. . . ." His eyes narrowed. "Didn't you say earlier that you're visiting family? Next thing you'll tell me, they run the fair."

She fumed in silence at his mockery.

"So which is it, Miss Mornay? Out visiting family or looking to find work?"

"*Both*—not that it's any of your concern. Now if you'll please give me back my case."

"Not a chance. I'm not letting you out of my sight, not till I know you're safe."

His words almost made her laugh with skepticism. *Safe? In the company of a Piccoli?*

"I'll be all right."

"What if they don't hire you? What'll you do then?"

She hadn't thought beyond asking for work. Hadn't even planned to look for work at the carnival, until his bullheadedness forced her into the excuse. But it wasn't a bad idea. In fact it was perfect. She needed more than two dollars, and with any luck she could locate her mother.

"That's what I thought." He answered his own question. "You haven't a clue what you'll do. Obviously you don't have more than that"—he nodded to the bills in her hand—"or you wouldn't have stowed away in my car."

Two long whistles shrilled through the night.

"You'll miss your train."

"I can take another."

"But what about your things? You might lose your baggage!"

"The porter will take care of what little I brought till I send a wire telling them where to deliver it. My family owns an interest in the railroad."

The news didn't surprise her.

"You're not getting rid of me so easily, Miss Mornay. Until I'm sure that you're out of danger, I'm sticking beside you every step of the way. My conscience won't allow otherwise."

" 'Out of danger,' he says," she grumbled beneath her breath, resuming her walk. "How'd a girl get to be so lucky?" And how could he talk about a conscience? His kind had none.

"I beg your pardon? I didn't hear you."

She gave him a sweet smile. "Since I can't shake your company, may we please continue, Mr. Piccoli? I'd like the opportunity to speak with the manager before they close."

"Of course, Miss Mornay." His smile was just as phony. He inclined his head. "For tonight, I'm your obedient servant. Please, lead the way."

She bit back a sharp retort. She was tired of arguing—her

entire day had seemed composed of it—and if he truly meant her harm, he'd had ample opportunity to act before now. Even here, in a dark field with no one the wiser, he seemed to show nothing but consideration for her welfare.

Maybe, just maybe, she could be wrong about his motives in helping her.

Don't fall for his smooth ways, logic warned.

Remembering the articles about his family, about him, she would indeed be foolish to think that a Piccoli entertained anything more than a selfish agenda. And she wouldn't be duped again.

❧

Roland had met plenty of dames by the time he'd turned twenty-three. Some smart, some dumb, a few falling a notch somewhere in between. But he had no idea what to make of this woman erroneously nicknamed Angel. Not that she wasn't as pretty as an angel; she was a real looker. And she could probably be sweet and pleasant if she tried. But she hadn't an ounce of sense in that sleek head of hers, and he felt more as if he'd taken on the role of her angel, her guardian angel.

He snorted at the preposterous thought of himself as an angel. Maybe a fallen one. She darted yet another wary and long-suffering glance his way, as if *he* were the chip on *her* shoulder.

He should just let her stumble her merry way through the field to the carnival, now that he'd diverted trouble for her a second time. But he couldn't bring himself to abandon the rash woman to whatever other dangers might await her recklessness. She reminded him of his sister, Gabriella—all spit and fire and independence, with no thought of where her hasty decisions could land her and no notion or experience of what to do when she got there.

He glanced at Angel's stiff profile. Perhaps he'd been too hard on her, calling her an ungrateful brat. He'd been relieved to spot her then alarmed to find her ringed in by a gang of street hoods, and he had allowed his exasperation with her to flame into ire once the danger had passed. His harsh words escaped before he thought twice; he didn't know her well enough to form opinions of her character. And she had thanked him, however curtly. Beneath the phony confidence she tried hard to exert, she was clearly alone and afraid. Grimly he plodded through the field of wild grass beside her.

"If we return to the station," he said again, "I'll buy you a ticket to wherever you want to go on the next train out of there. Only drop this screwy idea of joining the carnival. No telling what trouble you might find in a place like that."

"I appreciate the advice, but I've made up my mind."

"I've heard bad stories—"

"I'll be careful."

"I've yet to see that," he muttered beneath his breath.

"Listen!" She turned on her heel. "You don't have to hang around. No one's forcing you. By all means, go!"

"I already told you how I feel about leaving you out here all alone, so unless you're coming back to the station with me, you're stuck with my company, missy."

Drawing her mouth tight, she didn't answer. Roland reined in his frustration, realizing that talking to her like his kid sister wasn't helping. Finally they came to the fairgrounds. She asked a pretzel vendor where the owner was, and he pointed to a wooden ticket booth.

"Sorry, folks. We're closing for the night," the man said as they stepped up to it.

"Actually," Angel said, "I was hoping you might have a job available."

"You want a job?" The short, thin man with mustache and goatee beyond the brass grille window looked at Angel strangely, echoing Roland's thoughts. "At my carnival?" He looked from the luggage in her hand back to her face. "I can't pay much, with the nation's crisis being what it is."

"I don't need much."

"You running away from something, young lady?"

She hesitated, and Roland sensed it was because of his presence. "I'm looking for something," she said at last. "Something I think I can only find here."

The man, who reminded Roland of a dignified magician minus top hat and tails, raised neat eyebrows in surprise. "I'm not sure what you think you may find here, but my carnival isn't all fun and games. We take our work very seriously. If you haven't any intention of staying longer than a few weeks, it would be best for both of us if you'd just leave the way you came."

"Oh, I can be serious. Please, sir. I need the work."

He seemed to consider and held up a thick roll of tickets. "My ticket girl ran off two days ago, eloped with another one of my workers." He eyed her and Roland severely. "I can't have any funny business going on. I don't want to be left shorthanded again should you two not find the carnival to your liking and take it in your head to run off."

"Oh no! Y—you have it all wrong," she stuttered quickly. "I hardly know this man."

"Is that a fact?" He eyed her matching brown luggage still clutched in Roland's hand.

"Yes. We met on a train, and this. . .gentleman came to my aid." She hesitated with the word. "Please, give me a chance. I can sell your tickets. I'm good with managing money, and I get along well with people."

Roland held back a snort of disbelief.

"Well, you do have an enchanting smile," the owner drawled. "It helps to have beauty induce the tightfisted customers to loosen their wallets and buy more tickets." He looked her up and down. "But selling tickets won't be all that's required. Each carny helps raise and dismantle tents and engage in preparations at each destination where we entertain. Likewise we work together in daily chores. Can you cook?"

His words came fast, his question unexpected. She blinked, taken off guard. "A friend taught me how to do a number of things in the kitchen."

Roland wasn't sure why, but he had the feeling she exaggerated.

"Fifty cents a month comes out of your pay for board, another fifty for food. Like I said, I can't pay much. A dollar a week."

She winced but nodded. "That's not a problem."

"All right then, young lady, I'll give you that chance. The ticket girl who ran out on me was in charge of helping with breakfast. You'll also have that job. You can share a car with Cassandra. The living lot is the train at the back of the carnival. Her car is painted with a woman standing bareback on a white horse. Tell her Mr. Mahoney sent you. You start tomorrow, since this day is done." He locked up a small strongbox. "It'll be a relief to hand this job over to someone else and return to my office. If you need me, my car is at the head of the train."

"Thank you." Anxiety melted off her. "You won't regret this."

"Let's hope not."

She turned to Roland, looking a bit sheepish. "Thank you, too." She spoke under her breath so only he could hear. "I know I haven't been the best company, and I wasn't very nice when all you did was save me from that nasty situation earlier—both of them. But I'm not ungrateful. And I'm really not a brat." She gave him the first genuine smile he'd seen, stunning him, and reached for her large case, which he still held. "This time it really is good-bye. I hope you aren't late to wherever it is you were supposed to be." She nodded in farewell. Her luggage in hand, she walked down the midway toward the tents shielding the carnival train.

Flabbergasted by her change in attitude, Roland watched her go.

"Something more I can help you with, young fella? In case you forgot, we're closed for the night."

Roland came out of his semidazed trance and turned his attention to the owner.

Foolish. Crazy. Absurd. He could think of endless words to describe what he was about to do.

"You wouldn't happen to have another job for hire?"

Mr. Mahoney eyed the stylish cut of Roland's expensive silk shantung suit. "*You* need work? You're pulling my leg."

"Dead serious. I heard all you told Miss Mornay, about pay and board, and those numbers are fine with me."

The owner's sly smile warned Roland he wouldn't like what was coming. "Is that a fact?" the man drawled. "Well then, I might have just the sort of job for a strapping young fellow like yourself."

four

Angel knocked on the railcar and stepped back to glance at the near-life-size mural of a slim blond standing atop a white horse. When no answer came, she set her luggage down and worked to slide back the door.

"Hey! What do you think you're doing?" A woman's irritated voice came from behind, and Angel turned to find the painted image in the flesh, rhinestone costume, feathered tiara, and all. "That's my car you're nosing around."

Angel picked up her luggage. "Mr. Mahoney said I was to sleep here."

The woman eyed Angel up and down. "You're my new bunk mate? Hmm." Her reply left Angel clueless as to whether or not she passed muster when suddenly a smile lit the woman's face. "All right then. Come on in, and I'll show you around. I'm Cassie, by the way. Horse trainer and bareback rider extraordinaire. What do you do for an act?"

"I'm Angel. I was hired to sell tickets."

"That can be an act in and of itself, so I heard from Germaine. She was my bunk mate, now happily married and away from this joint. Watch your step. Let me give you a hand with those."

Angel gratefully accepted help with the luggage and grabbed both sides of the car to hoist herself up inside. Her new living quarters were sparse and cramped with two cots anchored one atop the other. But a row of sparkling sequin costumes hung in one corner, a woven blue and brown rug covered the floor, and a colorful oil painting of wild horses helped make things cozier.

"You're not planning on eloping, too, I hope?" Cassie teased, setting Angel's large case next to a small, mirrored dressing table. "Seems I just get a bunk mate broken in, and she leaves."

Memory of Mr. Mahoney's stern caution to her and the handsome rogue rescuer flashed across Angel's mind. That made two people in the span of ten minutes suggesting she might elope.

"I never plan to marry."

At her declaration, Cassie lifted one perfectly arched sable brow. "A pretty thing like you? Is that what you're running from, honey? An unwanted engagement?"

Angel stared back in shock at her accurate guess. "Running?"

"Nobody joins a carnival unless they're running from something or they were born into it, like me." She gave a bright smile. "I'm part of 'The Magnificent Death-Defying Hollars.'" She quoted the words painted on her railcar. "An act my parents started long before I came into the world. You might have heard of us?"

"No, sorry. I never went to carnivals as a child—that is, not that I can remember."

"Really?" Cassie looked at her as if she were a strange new bug. "Hmm."

"You've been with this carnival your entire life?"

"A good portion of it. My parents were part of a circus before the owners mismanaged it, and we came here."

Cassie's explanation led Angel to hope. "Then you know the sideshow acts?"

The pert blond laughed. "Honey, I'm well acquainted with all the carnies and showmen. From the vendor selling peanuts and pretzels, to the roustabouts, to the trainer of fleas." She blushed, making Angel wonder.

"Does a bearded lady work here?" Her question came out in a hopeful rush.

"A bearded lady?" Cassie tensed. "That's a rather odd question. You looking for one in particular?"

"Yes, as a matter of fact. She goes by the name of Lila. I'm. . ." She wondered how much to reveal and decided to be forthcoming. "I'm a relation."

Cassie regarded her with surprise. "Really?"

She didn't know it would be so difficult to say: "I'm. . .her daughter." The daughter she abandoned and wanted nothing to do with. Not for the first time, Angel wondered what compelled her to hope her mother's viewpoint might have changed.

"Her daughter," Cassie repeated softly, looking Angel over with curious shock before turning to the dressing table. Clearly she was amazed that Angel could descend from a woman with such an obvious flaw. Cassie sank to the stool. "I hate to disappoint you." She slipped off her feathered tiara, took a jar, opened it, and applied white cream to her thickly painted face. "No one like that works here now."

"Then she did before?"

"I wouldn't know." She moved her lower jaw to the side as she spoke, applying the cream, intent on her task.

Angel's expectations crumbled. "Perhaps she worked here years ago? I would have been with her. Fifteen or sixteen years ago maybe? I was only two, or three. . .I think. But she might have come back to join the carnival, though I'm not sure when. Maybe you might have seen her at some point these past few years?" Another ember of hope sparked. "Maybe she even told someone where she was going?"

Cassie busily set to work wiping off the cream with a cloth. "Sorry. I was just a little girl all those years ago. As for recently. . .sorry." She shrugged and set down the soiled cloth. "Other carnivals travel through the New England area, too. Maybe she's with one of them."

Devoid of the bold cosmetics, Cassie looked a great deal younger than Angel had first speculated, close to her own age. Maybe she really was too young to remember Angel's mother. Cassie swiveled around on the stool.

"Aw, don't look so glum." She smiled. "If it's meant to

happen, you'll find her. That's what Mama Philena says. If things are meant to happen, they will. You'll meet Mama tomorrow. She was a gypsy fortune-teller when the carnival first started but gave that up several years ago and has become a helper wherever she's needed and a mother to us all."

She delicately slapped her palms to her thighs, seeming nervous. Angel assumed Cassie also felt unsure around her new bunk mate. "Now, let me fill you in on the goings-on of Mahoney's Traveling Carnival and who and what you'll find here." Cassie stepped behind a half screen beside the rack of costumes. All the while she spoke of the "family," rustles and bumps came from the opposite side. Her head popped up now and then, followed by one shiny article of clothing after another, slung across the top of the screen. Her white hand appeared and fluttered to reach and pull a distant garment from a hanger. Angel stepped forward and grabbed the cotton wrapper, handing it to her.

"Thanks." Cassie soon stepped out, tying the wrapper around her waist. She ran a brush through her hair, the curls just touching her shoulders. "Most of us retire early, once the customers have gone home and chores are done. We rise before dawn. It's fun working in a carnival, but a lot of hard work goes into it to make it as entertaining as can be."

Not wanting to make any mistakes her first night there, Angel followed Cassie's example and changed into her bed gown behind the screen. She brushed her teeth and hair then regarded the bunks with uncertainty. Cassie set down the brush and looked in the mirror at Angel's image.

"Yours is the lower one. I prefer the top. Helps me keep in shape for my act."

To Angel's astonishment, Cassie swished around, jumped up, and darted toward the cots. She leaped upward like a gazelle, using her hand as a brace, her body forming a graceful sideways arc as she landed with ease atop her mattress, light as a feather. She grinned down at Angel, who gaped at her. "I know. I'm a hopeless show-off. It's just in the performer's blood, I suppose, and both my parents are Class A acts. Do turn down the lamp, won't you?" She breezed her long, slender body beneath the blanket and laid her head on the pillow. "Good night, Angel. Don't let the train bugs bite."

Angel chuckled and doused the light. She liked her bunk mate and hoped they might become good friends. Maybe she could find happiness here. . .and peace.

"You can't find peace in the world, child, till you find peace in your heart."

Nettie's words of wisdom drifted into her mind. She still didn't understand how her friend could believe in an all-loving and caring God, with so much suffering going on in the world. Still, it was Nettie's wise words, some of them verses from her Bible, that Angel had found herself clinging to on the difficult days. The only thing she regretted about her hasty flight was not saying good-bye to her dear friend.

❧

Standing alone inside the huge tent, Roland stared with dismay at the stalls of animals, wondering how his life had come to this.

Before him stood four beautiful grays, though they were not his problem. Their owner had just made it very clear he or his family would tend to all care of the champion horses. Three black ponies, assorted barnyard animals, and a baby elephant completed the unusual menagerie—all of them in his charge.

"Is this a circus or a carnival?" Roland directed his question to the wrinkled gray beast that stood almost as tall as he did. How in the world did one take care of a baby elephant?

"At least you know there's a difference," came a jovial voice from behind. "That's a start. Not everyone outside the carnival world does."

Roland turned to see a short, barrel-chested man with a

thin, waxed mustache and an infectious grin head his way. "I've been to both," Roland admitted.

"Impress me."

At the friendly challenge Roland took a guess. "A circus contains a variety of acts performed under a huge tent known as the big top. A carnival is a series of rides, games of chance, and sideshows along a midway, many of them rigged and containing acts of a far more sinister nature than anything one would find at a circus."

The newcomer raised his brows, not acting insulted by Roland's straightforward explanation that made clear this wasn't his first choice as a place to be. He'd had enough of *sinister* to last a lifetime.

"Okay, so I'm impressed." The man extended his hand, and Roland shook it. "You must be the new carny Mahoney hired. Pleased to meetcha. The name's Chester."

"Roland." He purposely left off his surname, relieved that Chester did as well, which prevented the need for excuses as to the omission.

"Nice to have you aboard, Roland. Mahoney told me you'll be sharing my car. My last bunk mate eloped with one of the ticket girls. It was his job Mahoney gave you."

"I'm overjoyed," Roland said in a monotone.

Chester laughed. "Aw, it's not so bad. Jenny here is docile as a lamb and easy to take care of, aren't you, girl?" He reached out and smoothed his hand over the elephant's coarse trunk. Jenny curled it in a gray U, aiming her snout toward Chester. "You know me too well. And you're getting downright spoiled, little lady." He rolled his eyes when Jenny made a soft trumpeting noise. "All right then, find the peanut." The end of her trunk pressed over his shirtfront then into the side of his jacket, slipping into a pocket. She fished the peanut out, with her trunk tip curled around the morsel, and brought it to her mouth.

"Cute trick."

Chester eyed Roland's own suit. "That's some sharp duds you got there." He quirked his brow. "Just why did you say you needed the work?"

"I didn't." Roland took no offense at his genial probing. If he were in Chester's shoes and a stranger showed up to work at a carnival wearing an expensively tailored suit, he'd wonder, too. "Long story," he hedged. "I'd rather not go into it."

"There's a number of those up and down the midway. Most of them hard-luck stories, with a number of us carnies hiding pasts we'd like to forget. Some shady, some not so much. You're right about your description of carnivals, though this one is private owned and also has shows and games acceptable for the kiddos. I'll give you the lowdown on what to avoid. For the most part, the performers and other carnies are a good bunch; you'll know soon enough who's a shyster. Isn't that right, Jenny?" He stroked her gray wrinkled head.

"Is Jenny part of your act?"

"*My* act?" Chester laughed. "No. Jenny here is a recent addition Mahoney & Pearson acquired. Her owner's an Arab kid. Doesn't speak good English, but he's nice enough. One of the circuses split up a few years back, and some of the acts signed on here." He patted the elephant high on the trunk again. "Me, I deal in the tiniest of critters in the animal kingdom, if you could call it that. I own a flea circus."

"Fleas?" Roland repeated in surprise. "You mean real, jumping fleas?"

"Don't use nothin' else, only mine don't jump. I heard of flea circuses that use tricks with magnets and the like, but my fleas are real enough. Nothing rigged going on in my tent. Come by sometime, and I'll give you a free show." He grinned. "You're not asking, but I see the question in your eyes: Why fleas? Well, it's like this: I like things small, in detail, and I like insects. My grandfather, he owned a flea circus at the turn of the century and taught me all he knew. But not to worry. Taking care of my fleas won't be on your list of duties," he joked.

"That's a relief. I may know the difference between a carnival and a circus, but to be blunt, I know little about taking care of animals—though the horse owner came in here a few minutes before you did and informed me to keep away from his."

Chester nodded. "Stan Hollar. Very particular about his property and who comes in contact with it. Those beautiful grays are Andalusians, some of the best horses you can find, and one of the top acts the carnival can boast. A member of the family checks in a few times a day, usually Cassie. I guess you could say Mahoney & Pearson counted themselves lucky when the Hollars signed on. They're one of the star attractions of the carnival." The wistful note to his voice led Roland to believe Mahoney wasn't the only one counting himself lucky.

"You about finished here?" Chester asked.

"I have no idea where to start. Mahoney just said to bed the animals down for the night."

"I grew up on a farm, so I'll give you a hand. Mama Philena usually comes to help out. Been with the carnival over thirty years. Mahoney's mama and like a mama to us all. She'll turn up eventually and show you the ropes."

Roland worked alongside Chester, grateful for the man's help and company. He didn't have friends or, rather, those associates he would call friends: men and women who were honest, loyal, and honorable. Most of the moral class, once they learned his name, assumed his family reputation went along with the label, which couldn't be further from the truth. Rather than destroy a possible friendship before it had a chance to build, Roland chose to keep silent about his identity. Angel knew, but he didn't think he'd have a problem convincing her not to share what she'd discovered.

That was, if she would talk to him at all once she realized he was here.

five

Angel woke up, found herself alone, and hurried to dress.

She met Cassie on the midway. "Sorry I overslept."

"That's okay," her bunk mate effusively greeted her. "Come on, I'll take you to the cookhouse tent." Soon they approached a structure composed of a canvas roof tied to poles. Two long tables stretched beneath, where the workers ate their meals.

"This is Angel," Cassie said in introduction to the few clusters of people who'd taken seats along the benches. "Say hi, fellow showmen and carnies, but you better be nice since she'll be preparing your breakfast in the future."

A sudden thumping shook a screen of canvas hanging beyond the tables as if a spoon had been whacked against it. "I'm still here, too, ya know!" came an unseen woman's grumpy voice.

A few of the men laughed. "As if we could forget," one of them muttered dryly. "Hello, Angel," more than several intoned, like a classroom of obedient schoolchildren.

"Hello," she said a bit shyly, darting a curious look toward the suspended canvas.

"Angel, my dear girl," a man said in a heavy British accent. "What a lovely name for a lovely face. As you are the latest connoisseur of food preparations, I should like to mention that I prefer my toast deeply browned and not blackened as the last girl chose to make it. I prefer the black to remain in my name."

A pretty, thickset woman with bleached hair and dark roots lightly slapped the wisecracking, balding man on the skull. "Be nice, Blackie. You heard Cassandra. She's new to

55

the family." The woman turned a big, toothy grin Angel's way. "Hiya, honey. I'm Ruth, and this here's my ball and chain, Blackie Watson."

"Now there's a spectacular idea, Buttercup. Incorporating a ball and chain into the act. A balloon that looks like a cannon, perhaps? Yes? Or even better, one bigger than a cannon. I would carry it like a deadweight then throw it at the children and set them to squealing."

"Whatever you think, dear." Ruth shook her head in mock exasperation, holding her hand straight out beside her mouth as if in confidence to Angel but hardly whispering, "Anything sets him off. Be careful what you say." She winked and lowered her hand. "We dress as clowns and perform up and down the midway, selling balloons to the kiddies."

Angel smiled in reply at the outgoing couple. Cassie took her beyond the sheet of hanging canvas that hid where food was being prepared. The delicious scent of warm oats she smelled upon arriving at the tent grew stronger.

"You're late!"

Angel winced, but Cassie smiled. "Millie, this is her first day. Be nice. Angel, meet Millie. Don't let her boss you around." She spoke to Angel with a teasing wink to Millie. "She's known for throwing her weight far and wide."

"You better just watch yourself, girlie." The grated tone belonging to the rail-thin woman didn't come across as amused. "Or you might find sand in your coffee 'stead of sugar."

Angel regarded the older woman with shock, but Cassie laughed. "We all joke with one another around here. You'll get used to us soon enough."

"Humph," the taciturn cook responded, but before Millie turned away, Angel thought she detected a smile on the worn brown face.

Cassie disappeared beyond the canvas. Angel wasn't sure what to say. She'd never lived in an environment that tossed around banter as a means to entertain and not hurt feelings. At her aunt's, she kept her thoughts to herself to avoid being criticized or having her feelings crushed. Still unsure of her footing in such a strange, new world, she kept silent, observing her fellow carnies.

Millie went back to work scooping creamy hot oats from a huge black pot and ladling the porridge into bowls. Angel was put in charge of making toast on a wire tray over the fire as Millie showed her. Since that was the sum total of food products Nettie had taught her to make, Angel felt relieved she wouldn't seem totally ignorant at her new job.

"We don't have a lot of the usual kitchen fare, as you can see, since you cain't very well pick up an oven and the pipes that go with it and move them 'round from place to place," Millie explained in her raspy voice. "There's a small stove on the train, but I do most of my cookin' over a slow fire. Like the rich flavor it brings. I can make any meal that goes in a pot. Cabbage stew. Potato soup. You name it; I can cook it. And when we have meat or poultry, they clamor for my pies." She beamed with pride as she poured coffee into tins that Angel then set on a tray to disperse among the carnies. As Angel worked, her initial nervousness dissipated, and she relaxed, enjoying her first morning there, even if she had yet to sit down and take her first bite.

She returned to the preparation area, tray empty, and refilled it with platters of toast, a rich golden brown, she noted with satisfaction. Concentrating on the success of her labors as she walked, she set the platter in the center of one end of the table.

"There you go, Blackie. Golden brown and not one speck of black, just the way you like it." She lifted her smiling gaze from the platter to where Blackie should be sitting. . .and inhaled so fast she thought she might choke, nearly swallowing her tongue.

The tall, dark stranger sat in Blackie's spot. Amusement danced in his rich dark eyes.

Blackie waved in acknowledgment to her from farther down the bench, where he'd taken another place at the table next to an extremely tall, bearded gentleman.

"Wh—what are you doing here?" she asked her persistent follower once she found her voice.

"And a good morning to you, Miss Mornay." Roland's straight white teeth flashed in a charming smile. "The toast looks delicious. Deep golden brown. And you're right— that's just the way I like it."

"I asked what you're doing here. This is where the workers eat. You shouldn't be here."

At her soft, insistent words, gritted through her teeth, those at that table quieted in curiosity.

"Actually, I should. I'm doing what every other carny is. Enjoying a hearty breakfast before taking on my duties."

"Your duties?" she gasped in mounting horror. For the first time she noticed his fine three-piece suit was missing. In its place he wore common clothes: a long-sleeved white cotton shirt, suspenders, and trousers like the other men, his lean, muscular build now apparent. But even with the change in clothing, he stood out from everyone else.

The gleam in his eyes was full of mischief. "Like you, Angel, I've joined the ranks of Mahoney & Pearson's traveling troupe. I'm a bona fide carny now."

☙

Roland watched without surprise as Angel made a quick excuse of being needed in the kitchen and hurried away as swiftly and gracefully as a kitten with a wolf in pursuit.

"She sure is jumpy," Chester observed from beside him. "You two have a history?"

"Not much of one and not like you mean it. A case of mistaken motives that started out in a series of awkward missteps. Truth is, I've known Miss Mornay less than twenty-four hours."

"You're joshing. With the way you two were staring at one another? No history whatsoever?"

"No history."

"Humph. Could've fooled me."

Roland decided it was high time to shift the focus off his life. "I happened to notice your eye wandering over to that pretty little blond sitting at the end of the bench." He glanced at the girl, who talked with another woman, similar to her in coloring and features, then looked back at his bunk mate.

Chester winced, and Roland noticed the flea man turn a shade red. "Cassandra Hollar. Part of the top act I was telling you about. That's her mother with her. And like her mom, Cassie's a bareback rider." His words grew wistful. "Best there is in all of New England, I imagine. All the world."

"I assume it's safe to say you two have a history together?"

"Nope. Her parents won't hear of it." Chester frowned, unusual to see on his effusive features. "They consider a flea trainer beneath them and unsuitable for their daughter."

"Tough break. She feel the same?"

"Hard to tell." Chester ducked his head, taking interest in his coffee. "Mahoney wants me to show you around after breakfast. Let you get a feel for the place."

"I'd like that." Roland looked toward the canvas, where Angel had disappeared. He thought she was taking a considerable amount of time to bring the next platter out and wondered if she was hiding from him.

&

"This is ridiculous," Angel chastised beneath her breath. "You can't hide behind this curtain forever."

"You say something?" Millie wanted to know.

"No, nothing." She gave her instructor a bright smile to hide her embarrassment at being caught talking to herself.

"Humph. You gonna take them bowls of porridge out or what?"

Angel straightened her backbone. She had escaped being trapped in an unfortunate marriage, had fled the everyday cruelties of her severe aunt and cousins, and had jumped aboard a train bound for a destination unknown to her in the dark of night. Surely she could muster up enough courage to again confront the grandson of the legendary crime boss who ruled half of New York City.

She swallowed hard. Then again, when she thought of it that way. . .

"Those bowls ain't gonna sprout wings and fly to the tables."

Angel nodded, determined. "I'm on my way."

The next few minutes went unpredictably well. Every now and then she sensed Roland watching her, but she avoided looking in his direction overly much. She would have preferred not to notice him at all, but his deep laugh as he talked with a couple of the carnies was both appealing and distracting and caught her attention more than once.

"Why does he have to be so disgustingly handsome?" she muttered as she sneaked a glance at him while gathering empty bowls as Millie had told her.

"Were you talking to me?" Cassie asked from behind.

"What?" she gasped, nearly dropping the dishes in shock. "No. I'm afraid it's a bad habit I acquired. Talking to myself, that is."

"If that's your only bad habit, Angel, you're as good as your name around here." The blond laughed. "As soon as you finish with breakfast, I'll take you on a tour of the midway to help you get acquainted with your new home."

"I'd like that, but I don't want to interfere with your work. You've already helped me so much. And I imagine I should find my way to the ticket booth soon, whichever one

Mahoney wants me at. I noticed there are a number of them all around."

"Oh, we have plenty of time. Relax. You need to eat, too."

Angel nodded and gathered her own food, taking a place far down the table from Roland and out of sight of him. Once she ate the bland but filling fare and the dishes and dining area were cleaned to Millie's satisfaction, Angel joined Cassie, who waited outside.

"Do you have anything casual to wear?" Angel's bunk mate asked.

"Will this not do?" She glanced at her navy skirt then at Cassandra's own denim trousers, knotted with a length of rope around her slender waist. "I don't own anything like that. My aunt wouldn't hear of it."

"I have a spare. I only wear them for manual labor—and you'll find there's a lot of that before the customers start arriving. Save your nice clothes for then."

"When is 'then'?"

"Early evening. Not much sense performing while the kiddos in school and the parents at work, those lucky enough to have jobs. We spend the mornings and afternoons rehearsing and working on new acts. On weekends we open in the early afternoon. I've found that every circus or carnival is different, each employing their own set of rules. And about those men you'll be working for—Pearson's a bit of a stickler, but Mahoney's a peach." She grinned. "He can be all bark and bluster, but he's really a sweetheart once you know him."

Inside their railcar, Angel changed into the denim trousers Cassandra lent her. She rolled them up at the ankles and belted them around her waist with a rope. Cassandra also lent her a man's work shirt. "Father gives me his cast-offs. No sons to bequeath them to." Cassie laughed, also tossing Angel a pair of flat-heeled shoes she had an extra pair of, which fit Angel surprisingly well.

As they left the railcar, Angel acknowledged the change felt better, warmer, and she didn't feel so out of place wearing men's clothes with Cassie dressed the same. Of course, had Aunt Genevieve seen her in anything other than a skirt or dress, she would have had a conniption fit. Angel smiled a little rebelliously at the thought, a smile that disappeared as both girls suddenly came face-to-face with Roland and a shorter man with laughing eyes.

Roland glanced at Angel's changed attire but didn't say a word. She wasn't sure if he approved or not, not that she cared.

"Hey, Cassie," the other man said. He stood as tall as she.

"Chester." Her greeting seemed shy.

"I was just taking Roland on a tour of the grounds."

"Funny. I was doing the same with Angel."

Barely glancing at Angel, he nodded in greeting. His eyes seemed hopeful as they again went to Cassie. "Well then, how about we go as a group? That way if one of us forgets something, the other can fill in."

Cassie darted a quick look around then nodded with an open smile. "Let's do that."

Angel's stomach dropped to her toes at this new arrangement. She couldn't exactly protest, since she did need to know the area and Cassie obviously wanted Chester to walk with them. During the next few minutes, however, the two leaders gravitated several feet ahead, walking together and leaving Roland and Angel to follow.

"I think they forgot about us," Roland said in amusement after minutes passed without either Cassie or Chester pointing out some attraction or sideshow tent along the midway, giving the new workers no more information.

"It does look that way." Her words came guarded.

He gave her a sideways glance. "I solemnly swear, on a stack of Bibles if you'd like, that I had nothing to do with this."

"No need to. This isn't a courtroom." She couldn't help

but see the irony, though. No matter which direction she chose to run to rid herself of his company—a closed door, storming away, sneaking off a train—somehow she always ended up back in his path. "But you can't say the same about finding work here. You meant to choose this place."

He hesitated. "You're right. I did."

"Then you admit it. You *are* following me." She stopped walking and whirled to face him in accusation.

He gave a gentle tug to her elbow. "Come on. We don't want to get left behind. They'd never know we were missing." They resumed their walk, and he released his light hold.

"Well?" she insisted after a few steps.

"What do you want me to say, Angel?" He sounded frustrated. "I wanted to make sure you were safe, especially after seeing those young thugs go after you. I know I said all this before, and call it none of my business, but finding you in my car and alone on the train, somehow that made it my business."

"I don't need a bodyguard."

"I don't think you know what you need."

Offended, she glared at him. "That's an incredibly judgmental statement to make, since you hardly even know me."

"You're right. But if we're going to talk snap judgments, you've done your fair share. Don't judge my character just because of my name, Angel. I'm not the terrible, preying villain you've made me out to be."

"You sure don't mind throwing your last name around to achieve your purpose!" She felt a little ashamed when she realized he'd done so only to help her, but she couldn't seem to back down.

He sighed, pinching the bridge of his nose. "I'm glad you brought that up. I'd appreciate it if you wouldn't tell anyone who I am. I'm just Roland here."

"Then you intend to stay?" She couldn't hide her distress. "There's really no need. These people are nice. Cassie,

Chester, Mahoney. I don't think I'll find trouble among this bunch, so don't feel obligated to remain on my account."

"Can we not argue, for once? We were coming close to getting along together on the train. Can we go back to that moment?"

"That was before you made me your personal mission." And before she learned he was a gangster. "I'm still not entirely sure of your motives."

"Okay." He released a weary sigh, throwing his hands up in defeat. "I confess. Joining the carnival did start out as a means to watch out for you, maybe even to get to know you better—"

"I knew it!"

"But that wasn't the sole reason. There's more to it than that."

She regarded him with skepticism. "How so?"

"I did a lot of thinking last night. You didn't ask what I was doing on the train, and I evaded your cousin's question about why I was in your hometown. Now I'll tell you, strictly in confidence, being as how only you know who I am and I'd like it to stay that way. But you must never tell anyone what I'm telling you. Do you understand, Angel? It's for your own good."

A sense of excitement mingled with dread at his overtly clandestine attitude made her nod slowly. She half expected a car of gangsters to suddenly careen into view, tommy guns firing.

He remained silent for so long she thought at first he had changed his mind about telling her. Their pace slowed, until they were even farther behind their tour guides and well out of earshot.

When he looked at her again, his expression was somber.

"I went there to visit the family of one of my grandfather's victims. A man who once worked for him. I went to see his wife."

Her eyes grew wide. "Who?" She scoured her brain for

all those in their small community who'd recently lost loved ones but struck a blank.

He shook his head slowly, his eyes grave, making it clear he wouldn't reveal that information. "For a long time I've wished to cut myself from the organization, from the family itself, but it's been nothing more than a hopeful desire and empty words on my part. Grandfather never believed I would follow through, and he was right. I tried to break away before but made half-hearted attempts at best. The life I led, it's all I know." He frowned. "Lately, more and more, I've detested what my family stands for and faced some hard choices. Do I turn a blind eye to the horror they generate and embrace the organization as I've been trained? Or do I listen to what's in my heart, telling me that such loyalty holds too steep a price, amounting to no good and leading only to regret, sorrow. . .and death."

Angel listened, sensing his pain ran deep. For the first time since they'd met, she felt a strange connection to Roland, who also suffered through his family for being different, and she sympathized with what he must have undergone and was still going through.

"I was on the train because I was also running, but God only knows where I was going. I sure didn't. Without my family's knowledge, I'd just met the young widow of the man my grandfather had bumped off for money owed. The poor man had three kids with one on the way. He was a dope for getting involved with my grandfather in the first place, but his widow is the one suffering. The whole stinking affair made me question if I wanted to return and take my so-called rightful place in the organization, as has been expected of me since I was born."

Wetness shone in Roland's eyes, and he hastily averted his gaze, blinking furiously. Moments passed before he again spoke.

"Then I met you. Courageous, full of purpose, ready to take

off alone in the night in a bold move to change what life threw your way. I may not agree with your methods, but I admire your spirit and independence, even envy it. You made a decision and were determined to follow through, no matter the obstacles. Watching you gave me courage to make my own getaway from family expectations, from the family itself."

She sensed him look at her. "I want to start over, Angel. To become my own man and somehow, if it's even possible, to redeem my family name. I never plan to spend another cent of their blood money, and that's one of two reasons I found a job here. I need the income, and they would never think to look for me at a carnival."

She snapped her focus his way. "You're in danger?" she whispered. "If they find you? Oh, but—surely your own family wouldn't harm you!"

His mouth tightened in a grim line. "My grandfather has a warped sense of right and wrong. A breach of loyalty to him and the organization is the same as treason to a king, even if it's morally the right thing to do. A cousin was rubbed out for having thought to be a squealer." His words grew vague, slow, as if he were speaking to himself and had forgotten her. She wondered if he'd ever aired his concerns to anyone before now. Somehow she doubted it and felt both honored and apprehensive that he confided in her.

He jerked out of his solemn musings and gave her a tight smile. "Grandfather would never believe I'd be working with a traveling carnival heading in the opposite direction from where I last told him I was going. Besides, he and his men wouldn't be seen dead in a place like this. Operas are his form of amusement, and nightclubs are his men's."

"But what if the troupe heads to New York City and someone recognizes you there? What then?"

"According to Chester, the carnival is traveling north through Connecticut. But if that day ever comes, if the train heads for New York, I'll figure out a plan of action then."

She nodded, trying to sort through the startling weight of his disclosure.

"Hey." He stopped and pulled her around to face him, resting his hands lightly on her shoulders. "I didn't tell you any of this to upset or worry you. You're safe, even if they find me, which they won't. I only told you to set your mind at ease that I'm really not stalking you and do have a good reason for being here. Okay?"

She returned his faint smile. "I'm not sure. Does this mean you've finally quit your job as my guardian angel?"

He snorted in mild displeasure at the term, dropping his hands to his sides. "An angel? No. But you could do worse than have me for a bodyguard. I've been trained all my life to be alert and cautious, among other things." He didn't elaborate, and she decided she didn't want to know.

"I suppose then, it's okay," she said on a mock sigh. "But I really can take care of myself." She couldn't resist the reminder, and he laughed.

Shivers danced along her spine at the warm, spontaneous sound. For a reason she couldn't grasp, especially after such grim revelations, she felt buoyant as they caught up to their hosts. Chester and Cassie once again remembered they had company and turned to tell Roland and Angel about the next attraction.

Upon seeing the sideshow tent and the banner above it, Angel froze.

six

Roland wondered what had happened. One minute they were finally talking on companionable terms, and the next, Angel seemed to have turned to stone.

"Are you all right?" he asked in confusion.

"Fine," she whispered, her eyes on the banner that hung high and spread from one end of the wide tent to the other. "Just. . .fine."

Roland looked up at the painted caricatures displaying all manner of human oddities lined up in a row, six of them, from a tattooed man covered in pictures and piercings to a pair of Siamese twins joined at the shoulder.

"The Human Freak Show," Chester read. "One of the carnival's main attractions. That and Cassie's act probably bring in the most money."

"More's the pity," Cassie intoned. "It's a shame to parade people around as if they were nothing more than animals."

Angel threw a swift look her way but didn't respond.

"I never noticed any of them at the cookhouse tent," Roland observed.

"They don't eat with the rest of us, except for Jim the Giant—the tall man who sat at our table," Chester explained. "He stands at near seven feet and sure is handy when I need something retrieved that's out of reach. I'm a tad on the short side, you might have noticed," he joked. "A likable fellow, Jim. Don't know the others. The man in charge of the sideshow keeps them hidden for the most part. He has a black soul, I'd wager, and doesn't treat them at all well."

"Then why do they stay?" Angel's words were hoarse. She stared at the tent.

"My guess is they have no other way to make a living. They're ridiculed by society and, especially in these hard times, wouldn't risk leaving a place that offers sure room and board. Back in the nineteenth century, things were worse. Their kind were thought of as monsters and put in cages. Some of them were even hunted down and killed."

Angel winced. "But some leave, don't they?" Her question seemed far from casual. "Some leave this carnival world and go on to lead normal lives?"

Chester scratched his head. "I suppose so."

"Do you know anyone from this carnival who did?"

"Can't say as I do. But I've only been with Mahoney & Pearson a little over a year."

"I'd like to meet them. . .the ones who work inside that tent."

Chester raised his brows in surprise. Even Roland looked at Angel oddly upon hearing the resolve that strengthened her melancholy words. Cassie's gaze went elsewhere, past the tent to the stationary Ferris wheel; she seemed to have detached herself from the conversation.

"I'm not sure that's possible," Chester said. "You'd need to talk to Tucker, the man in charge, and he's not a nice sort. Another thing, they might take offense to your asking them questions. For the act, they do as they're told, but for the most part, they keep to themselves and don't trust others. Can't say I blame 'em."

"I'd still like to try," Angel insisted softly.

"Just why are you so interested?" Chester asked.

Angel shrugged, but Roland sensed she was hiding something. "If they don't want me there, I'll go. I'd just like the chance to meet and talk with them. Not to. . .observe them."

"Tell you what I can do," Chester relented. "After my act some night, assuming you can find someone to man your ticket booth, I'll take you to the last show. Afterward, I'll talk with Tucker and pass along your request."

"Thank you, Chester. I'd appreciate that."

Roland felt Chester could be trusted but didn't like the idea of Angel going anywhere alone with the man. Judging by Cassie's slight frown, neither did she.

"We should be going," she urged. "There's more to see and do, and I have to get to work soon. I need plenty of practice if I want to try out my new act this weekend."

"Not the backward flip?" Chester didn't sound pleased.

"Exactly that."

"You almost got yourself killed last time!"

"I've been working on it. I have the timing down now."

The two moved toward the midway, quietly arguing.

Roland wondered what existed in women that their entire gender seemed to think they could face any risk and get away with it, as if supposing they could exercise complete control over its outcome. He'd never been dense enough to assume he had control over his life; his father and grandfather wielded supreme authority and rarely gave him the chance to think for himself. His little sister, on the other hand, possessed a streak of confident carelessness; Cassie obviously thought herself indestructible, and Angel foolishly entertained the same theory.

But it wasn't her string of reckless acts that concerned him at the moment. She continued to stare at the banner, her eyes full of horrified pity mingled with grief and. . .tears?

"Angel?" he quietly prodded.

She looked his way as if just coming out of a trance.

"Maybe we should catch up with the others?"

"Okay." She whisked away the moisture that beaded her lower lashes.

"Hey, what's wrong?" He hadn't expected the low blow to his gut that the sight of her tears caused him.

She shook her head as if she wouldn't answer then did.

"Do you ever wonder where they come from?" she asked sadly. "About their families, and if they, if they. . .miss them?"

"Homesick?" he asked gently. "Wish now you'd never taken the train? You can still go back, you know."

"No." She gave one last somber glance to the banner. "I can never go back." Turning from him, she walked away.

Curious at her hollow words, Roland watched her a moment before moving to catch up to her. "Then it looks like there's nothing left but to make the best with the hand you've been dealt."

A slight grin tilted her mouth. "That sounds like something Nettie would say. Except for the gambling part. She abhorred it. Said it was the devil's game."

"Nettie?"

"My aunt's cook and a very dear friend. If she were here right now, she'd probably tell me that, in order to stay strong, I must face the day so that the shadows are behind me." At the puzzled lift of his brows, she clarified, "When you face the sunlight, shadows fall behind you. It was her way of saying not to live in the past or dwell on where you've been."

"Smart lady, your cook. Wish it were so simple."

"It's really not, is it? Sometimes the past leaves questions that need to be answered—"

"Hey, you two," Chester called back. "Are we talking to ourselves up here? I thought you wanted a tour."

"We're coming." Angel quickened her pace. Roland regretted that she'd had no chance to continue and hoped they might resume their conversation later.

The rest of the tour proved more peaceful. Angel didn't talk much, but she relaxed, laughing at Chester's jokes and giving Roland more than one of her pretty smiles in reply to something he said. He felt relieved that she obviously no longer resented or feared being in his company. The four parted ways at Chester's tent, with an invitation and promise to come view his act soon.

"Maybe we can talk again later?" Roland suggested to Angel once Cassie headed for the back of the lot, where the biggest attractions stood, and Chester disappeared inside his tent.

Peering up at him, she squinted, as if thinking it over. "Maybe we can." She gave him an easy smile and walked in the direction opposite where the animals lodged.

Roland watched her go. And maybe. . .joining up with the carnival would offer bonuses he'd never dreamed of. He couldn't say if he desired Angel as a potential girlfriend, even as a date. That was thinking too far ahead, and his state of affairs was shaky at best, disastrous at worst. But he would like to know her better, and it seemed, for once, she agreed.

He found it a frightening prospect, but freeing as well, not having to answer to the immoral traditions of the Piccoli way of life. And this time he was determined to make it last.

❧

After hours of standing on her feet, Angel made her painful walk to the car she shared with Cassie. In the narrow ticket booth by the Ferris wheel, there hadn't been a stool on which to sit, though there was room for one. She enjoyed the lively music that rang through the evening, hour upon hour, and the children's happy laughter and squeals, but she envied those customers who sat in the little hanging cars. She would have been content to sit on the ground by the time she closed. At least the living lot wasn't far.

Once inside her railcar, she slipped off her pumps and wiggled her toes, lifting hot, swollen feet to the mattress where she half reclined. Cassie wasn't there yet, and she took the opportunity to pull her valise from beneath the bunk, rummage for the album, and bring it to rest on her pillow. She found the photograph and ran inquisitive fingers over the faded image of the veiled face.

"Who were you, Mother?" she wistfully asked. "What did you feel. . .think? Why'd you give me away? Because of your face? Or did you even want me to begin with?"

A swift thump against the outside wall of the railcar startled her. She shut the book and sat up, almost banging her head on the bunk above. When the door didn't swing open, revealing Cassie, she grew curious and went to investigate.

Outside, a man with wild sandy brown hair leaned with one fist against their car. He looked her way, his hazel eyes snapping in anger.

"Whatta you want?" He pulled his hand from where he'd slammed it, making a clear effort to try to regain control over whatever upset him.

"I'm Angel. I live here." She hesitated then stepped down. "I heard a noise."

"Angel, is it? Yeah, I heard about you." He ignored her reference to his action. "I'm one of them who runs the gaming booths—Harvey's the name. My car's behind yours."

"Oh." She smiled politely. She knew the car ahead of theirs belonged to Cassie's parents, briefly wondered where Roland slept, then wondered why she should care.

"It's a pleasure to meet you," she said quickly, to cover up her flustered state over the thought of Roland so suddenly entering her mind.

Harvey's brows sailed up. "You might change your tune in time. I'm told I'm not easy to get along with." He shook his hand a bit. She noticed the knuckles were red and scraped.

"We all have our moments. Is your hand all right?"

He slipped the offended member into his jacket pocket. "Not a thing wrong with it."

His tone suggested she was prying, and she prepared to tell him good night, when the crunch of footsteps made her look behind. After all she had experienced with her rescuer rogue, it didn't surprise her to see her visitor.

Roland looked from Harvey to Angel. "Am I interrupting?"

"Just meeting my neighbor." Angel grew irritated. She'd thought after their last conversation he would stop snooping into her affairs, that they were on their way to relating on good terms. But he obviously hadn't quit his self-assigned role as her guard.

Roland looked the man up and down as if he'd like to eliminate him. "Name's Roland."

Harvey crossed his arms over his chest and narrowed his eyes. "You're the new fellow they got to look after the animals."

"I am." It sounded like a challenge.

"Don't like animals."

"How was your first day?" Angel asked quickly, hoping to defuse a potentially volatile situation.

Roland's taut features relaxed a bit as he looked her way. "For someone just learning the ropes, good, I suppose. Mama Philena was a big help. Have you met her yet?"

"I've heard about her."

"You'll like her. She's a character." He gave Harvey another once-over before again directing his attention to Angel. "How was your day?"

"Long, exhausting. I managed."

"Well, I'll just let you two get on with your little chitchat," Harvey said snidely. "I haven't the time." He moved toward his railcar without waiting for a reply.

"Nice fellow," Roland said dryly. "A new friend?"

His tone exasperated her. "What if he is? Are you going to disapprove and tell me I should stay away from him? That he's too dangerous?"

"Just asking."

She doubted it and tilted her head with suspicion. "Just why are you here, Roland?"

"Excuse me?"

"You must have come for some reason other than to reveal

your displeasure with the company I keep." She wasn't really keeping Harvey's company but didn't bother to tell him that.

"Actually, I was heading to my car." He moved past her.

"Your car?"

Her stunned words stopped Roland in his tracks, and he turned to look. "You didn't think I was bedding down with the animals, did you? As a matter of fact, we're neighbors, too. My living quarters are next door to your new friend's." He tipped his hat. "Good night, Angel. I'll see you at breakfast."

She stood speechless, stunned that her curiosity had been so promptly satisfied. The train wasn't the longest she'd seen, but she didn't think he would be so close. It didn't irritate her, exactly, but it did unsettle her, making her stomach take a sudden sharp dip.

"Hi, Angel," Cassie's voice broke through her thoughts as Angel watched Roland retreat into the second car down from theirs. "What are you doing out here?"

"Talking to the neighbors." She noticed Cassie's puzzled scan of the now-empty area. "Did your stunt work?"

Cassie scowled. "Papa's being stubborn and won't let me try it out on the crowds yet. But I have half a mind to anyway. How was your first day?"

"Busy. Hardly got a chance to breathe."

"Not surprising. The rides are a huge draw." Cassie grew excited. "Say, I can ask Mahoney to let you work the ticket booth by our tent. That way you could slip in and watch me perform sometime."

"That would be great, only. . ."

"What?"

"Can I have a stool in the booth?"

Cassie laughed. "The ground not so soft on your poor pups?" She cast a glance down to Angel's stockinged feet as she opened the door of their railcar and swung up.

Angel followed. "That, and the heels of my pumps. It's

muddy there. If it's all right with you, I'd like to wear the flats again."

"Sure. Keep them."

"Thanks." Angel slid the door on its track to close it but couldn't resist poking her head out one last time.

She didn't really expect Roland to be standing outside, did she?

Shaking off such silly thoughts and an even sillier twinge of disappointment, she firmly shut the door.

seven

As Roland worked, he thought about the grubbiness of his current task. Strange that as menial and dirty as his new job was, he felt cleaner than when he'd dressed to the nines and kept an account of his grandfather's books, which had been the nicest of his worst assignments.

"So when are you going to marry the girl?"

At Mama Philena's outrageous words, Roland almost dropped the long-handled brush he held. He looked inside the tent toward the nearest stall. "Excuse me?"

"You heard." She looked to where he stood outside with Jenny, giving her a bath. "It's obvious you're smitten and the two of you have something going on."

Somewhere in her sixties, Mama, as the carnies all called her, stood two feet shorter than Roland and had more brass than he'd seen in men twice her size. With her gray ringlets pulled back by a bright ribbon and wearing the most vibrant colors in clothing he'd seen—today's choice an eye-straining orange and violet—Mama was unique. She had a habit of squinting, as she did now, and Roland wondered if the woman needed corrective glasses as well as an alteration in judgment.

"I've known her three days."

"Could have fooled me. I can read people well, son. It's why I took a job as fortune-teller when I was young, when Mahoney's papa, my husband, ran the place. I knew nothing about looking into crystal balls and that sort of nonsense—didn't believe in it then; don't believe in it now. Just all for show. Gave the air of mystery the customers clamored for. But I could look into a person's eyes, watch their body language, and read their emotions easy. If they were sad. Happy. Nervous. Figuring out a fortune to match wasn't hard."

"Why'd you quit?"

"I got convicted."

"Convicted?" He stopped sweeping the brush along Jenny's hide.

Mama finished currying one of the Andalusians. Apparently the owners gave her free rein when it came to their beautiful beasts, unlike Roland, whom they watched as if he might suddenly set their horses' tails on fire. In the short time he'd been with the carnival, he'd learned that few crossed this feisty woman.

"A funny thing, that." She set the brush down on a sawhorse bench, growing pensive. "A few years back, a carny who worked here, she did the convicting. Told me about God and His love. Said a woman once came to see her act and witnessed to her—that was the word she used—'witnessed.' Funny word.

"Puts me in mind of someone being sworn in to tell the whole truth and nothing but at a trial. In a sense, I guess that's what it is. Plenty of people tend to act nervous and strange, like felons, when you tell them of God—much like they do in a courtroom, I expect. She said she wanted to spread His message and do for others what that woman had done for her. Sweet woman but so sad. And not just because of her appearance. . . ." Her words trailed off, as if she relived the moment or realized she'd said too much; Roland couldn't be sure. "Listen to me, carrying on when we have a full morning's work! How's Jenny's bath coming along?"

Roland's attention returned to the baby elephant that had begun to fan her ears and sway her immense body, a sign he'd come to understand as her becoming agitated. "It would help if Jabar was here. I think Jenny wants her master. She doesn't seem happy with me."

Mama let out a little huff of exasperation. "That boy can never seem to be anywhere on time, and having his arm in a sling doesn't help. Poor dear. We warned him not to climb on top of the train, but he just doesn't listen, or maybe it's that his English isn't good so he didn't understand. At least the fall only sprained his arm instead of breaking it—or his fool head."

Roland had been surprised to learn Jenny's owner was a ten-year-old Arab orphan whose parents died in a fire. What didn't surprise him was how Mama coddled him, a nurturing mother hen to an adopted lost chick.

"Hullo!" a boy's cheery voice called, and Roland turned to look. His heart jumped a sudden beat at the sight of the two approaching.

"Speak of the little devil," Mama murmured affectionately, exiting the tent.

"I brought pretty lady," the scamp continued, his black eyes twinkling merrily beneath his white turban at Roland. "She must see you."

Angel's skin flushed deep rose, her eyes flashing to Roland in embarrassment then settling on Mama. "Actually, he got that mixed up. I came to talk to you. Mr. Mahoney said he needs you. He also said you could tell me where to find a stool for the ticket booth."

"That boy of mine couldn't find an elephant in a pup tent," Mama quipped and patted Jenny's flank. "Isn't that right, Jenny?"

Jenny stood at attention, the snout of her trunk merrily roaming Jabar's front then curling around his slim hips. He fed her a peanut. "Up, Jenny! Up!" he commanded with a smile.

The elephant obeyed, lifting her agile owner, who couldn't have weighed more than Angel's satchel, high into the air and over her head, while the boy sat perched in the curve of her trunk. As Jenny loosened her trunk from around the boy, he stretched one skinny brown leg over the top of the elephant, nimbly swinging around to sit astride the animal.

Roland had watched but still couldn't figure out how the boy did it. Jabar beamed at the two new carnies staring up at him in awed disbelief. Roland shook his head and glanced at Angel. She looked his way, grinning, then shrugged.

"Jabar, you shouldn't be showing off any tricks with your arm in that sling," Mama reprimanded.

"Jenny not hurt Jabar. Jenny love Jabar." He leaned forward and patted the elephant's head.

"That may be, but that doesn't have anything to do with— oh, never mind," she finished in frustration when the boy quirked his head, puzzled, as if unable to follow her words. "Just be careful. We wouldn't want to put both your arms in slings, now would we?" She turned to Angel. "About that stool. Chester might have a spare. I remember seeing more than one in his tent. Roland, why don't you go along and carry it for her?"

"Oh really, that's not necessary—"

"I'd be happy to."

He looked at Angel as they both answered at once. "That is, if you don't mind the company."

Her lips lifted a fraction, and he felt relieved he had guessed right to give her the choice instead of choosing for her.

"I suppose not."

At her soft response, Mama chuckled and muttered, "Oh no, nothing going on there at all!"

Roland ignored her smug comment and brought his fingertips to Angel's elbow long enough to turn her toward Chester's tent and away from Mama's suggestive musings.

"What did she mean?" Angel gave him a sidelong glance as they walked down the midway.

"Did she say something?"

"Now Roland." Her voice took on the tone of an amused scolding. "You know she did."

"Sorry. Wasn't paying much attention, what with—"

"Hey! Watch out."

Startled to hear a childish shriek from near the ground, they looked down. But it wasn't a child who stood there, though the voice sounded as if it belonged to one. A dwarf woman in her twenties, the blue feather she wore in her hat half her approximate three feet of height, stared up with china blue eyes, her hands balled on her hips. Blond ringlets spilled from beneath her hat to her tiny shoulders.

"You can say that again—about not paying attention," she huffed. "You two trying to mow a person down?"

"Sorry!" Angel said. "We didn't see you. That is, I mean. . ." She blushed furiously at her thoughtless words, but the woman only chuckled and lowered her hands.

"That's all right, honey. I expect if I were ten feet tall, you wouldn't have seen me either, not with the way you two were staring at each other. So, you two are the new carnies I've been hearing so much about. Coming here together and pretending not to know one another?"

"Oh, but we didn't! It wasn't how it looked—"

"I got eyes." The woman interrupted Angel's flustered re-mark and winked. "My name's Posey." She struck up her hand. "As in pretty as a posy. That's what my sweetheart says." She smiled shyly, revealing two dimples.

"I'm Angel." She bent down to take the offered hand. The woman gave Angel's a swift shake then turned to Roland, doing the same as he introduced himself.

"Just don't let Mahoney know there's anything going on between you two, you being so new here and all. He's still upset Germaine and Lionel left him high and dry."

"But really, we're not together—"

Posey looked beyond them. "Oh, there's my sweetheart now!" She smiled. "Would you like to meet him?"

"Of course," Roland inserted, aware of Angel's distress

over the misconception of their relationship.

A young man no taller than Posey, with dark red hair and blue eyes, came up beside her. "How's my darlin' Posey today?" he asked, an Irish lilt to his accent. He gave her a kiss on her dimpled cheek. Suddenly shy, she clutched her hand in her skirts and batted her lashes.

"Oh Darrin. These are the new carnies. Angel and Roland."

"You two married?" Darrin asked.

Angel gasped in outright shock, and again Roland answered. "Just friends." She didn't correct him, and he felt thankful that maybe he wasn't assuming too much to say so.

"That's how me and Darrin started off," Posey said, dreamily looking into his eyes. "We fought like cats and dogs at first, always snapping at each other, but one day something just clicked. We're getting married two weeks from now." She directed her happy gaze up to Angel. "You'll come to the wedding, won't you?"

Roland didn't miss Darrin's sharp look at Posey.

"I'd love to." Angel found her voice.

"I would, too." Roland felt Angel glance at him then away again.

"Oh good!" Posey beamed.

"But I'm surprised Mr. Mahoney will allow it," Angel said, "after all I've heard about his view on carnies getting involved."

"Mahoney knows a gold mine when he sees one. We're staying with the carnival. Our manager has already tagged us as 'The tiniest leprechaun couple to walk the face of the planet.'" She rolled her eyes. "As long as it snags the crowds, they don't mind what we do."

"Don't know the truth of that, us being the tiniest," Darrin added. "But let them have their fun, as long as they let us have ours. Right, Posey me love?"

She giggled like a besotted schoolgirl. "Right, my darling

prince. We should be getting back to the tent. So nice meeting you both. Come on, honey." She took hold of Darrin's hand, pulling him away with her.

"Are you certain you should have invited them to our wedding?" Roland heard Darrin ask as the two walked away.

"Hush! They'll hear. And Mama was right. They're nice, not like some who joined up. I heard Angel's even been asking to speak with us—"

"More like gawk at us."

"You aren't used to that yet?" she scoffed. "Anyway, I like her. And she was gawking because you asked if they were married. Fine thing! She was all right before you did that. For whatever reason, they want to keep their little affair a secret, so let them. . . ."

Angel's eyes widened as she looked after the tiny couple, now out of earshot. *Affair?* she mouthed and swung her annoyed gaze to Roland's.

He wasn't sure whether to apologize or excuse himself and seek escape.

"This is your fault," she seethed. "You insisted on following me here, and now the entire carnival thinks we're headed for the altar or are already married and hiding it. I've been hearing remarks like that for days."

"And because I insisted on following you here," he responded levelly, "those young hooligans didn't try to come back and finish what they had started."

"They probably wouldn't have come back at all."

"You can't guarantee that. I know the type, remember."

"How could I forget?" she responded sweetly, her eyes filleting him where he stood.

"I wish you would."

At his quiet words, she clamped her lips tight, glancing away.

"Would it be so bad for them to think I happen to like

you and want to see more of you?"

Her eyes snapped up to him again. "I told you once before, I'm not a loose woman, and I won't be thought of that way!"

"No one thinks that."

"An *affair*?" she reminded incredulously.

He winced at how vile she made the word sound. "Posey's colorful vocabulary. You met the woman. She'd probably call a dame blinking her eyes as being cast under a witch's spell."

"Could you please not use that word?"

Her unexpected switch caught him off guard. "What word? *Witch*?"

"*Dame*. I don't like it. It sounds. . .cheap."

Roland had never associated the word as meaning anything but a lady. Everyone he knew used the slang term, but he nodded. "If it'll make you happy, I'll stop."

His quick acquiescence mollified her. "I'm sorry I jumped on you. I suppose it really isn't your fault how they perceive us."

"You're upset. It's understandable. If I hadn't insisted on carrying your luggage, you're right, they wouldn't have immediately paired us off." Word of mouth obviously spread fast through the carny grapevine. "But again, is it really so bad for them to think we might happen to like each other?"

Her eyes widened. "Do you?"

"Like you? Yes."

She looked away as if suddenly at a loss, and he resisted the strong urge to ask if she returned the favor or at least no longer considered him the enemy.

"We're attracting attention." She released a weary breath, and he glanced around, noticing a few workers had stopped what they were doing to stare. "Let's walk. To Chester's tent, I believe it was?" She resumed moving down the midway.

Roland fell into step beside her, casting her sidelong glances. He wanted to know how his admission made her feel, but this was the worst possible time to broach the subject. If he tried, she might push him into the wall of the tent they now passed then run off as the whole thing came tumbling down on top of his head.

They arrived at Chester's tent just as Cassie rushed out of it. Dashing her fingers beneath her eyes shining with tears, she appeared more than a little upset.

"Cassie?" Angel asked in concern.

The blond shook her head, her face a picture of complete distress. "I don't want to talk about it." She hurried away.

Angel looked after Cassie, as if uncertain what to do, then glanced up at Roland. He shrugged and shook his head, defeated when it came to a woman's tears. He could barely figure out the woman with him, much less a near stranger. Even though the woman with him was almost that. So why, then, did he feel a connection to her, experience an urge to protect her, and battle an almost-constant desire to be with her?

Curbing a groan, he held the tent flap aside and allowed her to enter Chester's tent ahead of him.

❧

Chester offered them both an abrupt nod in greeting, his jaw tense. Angel had never seen the affable man look so sullen. She considered asking if everything was all right between him and Cassie but decided not to interfere. She didn't know him well enough to invite confidences.

"Hope we aren't intruding," Roland said.

Chester shrugged, the smile he offered grim. "What can I do for you two?"

Angel told him about her need for a stool, and he readily complied.

"Sure, I can let one go." He moved to a wooden counter where three stools sat in front of what looked like a miniature circus, smaller than a dollhouse. Tiny striped tents and banners stood erected on a platform. A model of a Ferris wheel, half the size of her hand, stood to the side.

Fascinated, Angel drew near. "Did you make this?"

"Sure did." A bit of tension drained from his voice.

"It's very good. There's so much detail." She sensed Roland draw closer, though he maintained his distance.

"As long as you're both here, why don't I give you that free show? I haven't much else to do, so come see my little beauties." His manner undergoing a complete roundabout, Chester looked beyond Angel's shoulder with a grin. "Come on, Roland, my man. Step right up. Don't be shy." He moved to retrieve a cigar box and carefully slid back the lid.

Angel heard Roland's footsteps rustle nearer in the grass.

Chester put something from his hand onto the small carnival layout. He looked up again.

"You'll have to come closer. These human fleas are small. You'll need to look at them through the special Fresnel lens I have."

Angel inhaled softly as she felt Roland's warmth at her back, though no part of him touched her. She struggled to concentrate on what Chester said as he showed each of his fleas' amazing tricks. One appeared to lift a set of barbells, another to pull a wagon. A third to dance. Another flea moved the Ferris wheel by walking atop it.

"That is amazing," she said, genuinely impressed. "You called them names, but how do you tell them apart?"

"Waltzing Matilda is faster than the others. Slow Moe at the wheel, well, his name tells it all. Each of them has a different personality or characteristic."

She bent over the lens again. "They're so tiny! What do they eat?"

"They don't call them human fleas for nothing."

She straightened. "Wha—oh."

"Yeah, Cassie had that same horrified look in her eyes when she found out. Ever been bit by a mosquito? Dozens at once? Not much different, except I know my beauties haven't any diseases, since I take care of them. Sadly, their life span is short though. Doctors used to use leeches, and my little gems don't take anywhere near as much blood as one of those."

Unable to prevent a little shudder, Angel looked into the lens again. The sudden stirring of her hair by Roland's warm breath as he also leaned in to look had her jump as high as one of the fleas.

She straightened, knocking into him, and twisted around, startled to find him so close. His dark eyes stared into hers, only inches away. It took a moment for her mind to start functioning again.

"I imagine you want to see, too." She hastily stepped aside. "Please, take my place. I must be getting back. Thanks for the free show—and the stool." With a tense smile, she picked one up and escaped from the tent.

"She's got it bad," Chester said with an annoying chuckle.

"I don't think so."

"Then you're blind, deaf, *and* dumb." His words came calmly as he began putting away his flea family. "And I don't mean mute."

"Don't I get a look?"

"You're not going after her?"

"It's the last thing she wants."

"I wouldn't be so sure. Cassie behaved like Angel, too, at first."

Since he opened the topic, Roland pursued. "And now? She didn't look happy coming from your tent."

Chester's jovial features tightened into their earlier grimace. "Daddy problems. Someone told him they saw us together, and Cassie got a reprimand."

"I don't get it. She looks old enough to choose for herself and not have to worry about her parents doing it for her."

"Yeah, but she respects her father and his wishes. Crazy

thing is, I actually admire that, as aggravated as it can make me. You, on the other hand, don't have a disapproving father to worry about. So get on out of here and find Angel."

"What about my free show?"

"I'm not going anywhere; neither are the fleas. But she is." Chester inclined his head toward the exit. "Go on." He resumed putting the fleas in the box.

"Fine."

Roland left Chester alone with his flea family. Angel was right. The whole blasted carnival seemed ready to pair them together, not that he minded. But he had more chance of riding atop an elephant and learning Jabar's tricks than he did of discovering the secret to talking with Angel on pleasant terms, and that's what infuriated him. The carnies' wisecracks and sly glances only added salt to the wound of Angel's indifference.

Roland had never classified himself as arrogant or conceited. Young women his family approved of had shown interest in him, his money, his name, but he never really took part in anything serious. He would be lying if he didn't admit that Angel's disinterest didn't sting a little—all right, more than a little. And maybe it was one part challenge and five parts concern that prodded him to find opportunities to share her company. But the most peculiar feeling had come over him, especially lately, that the reason for her frosty attitude had to do with more than Roland being a Piccoli. She was hiding something; he was sure of it.

Up ahead, he spotted her and held back, his muscles again going tense when he saw the carny from the night before with her. What was his name? Oh yes. *Harvey*.

Roland didn't want to behave like her shadow, stalking her, and he sure had no claim on her life or reason to be jealous. But when the crude man grabbed her elbow, once she moved away, he felt his hands curl into fists and just prevented himself from lunging forward. He waited, watching to see what she would do.

She glanced over her shoulder to where the louse held her, said something, then snapped her arm from his hold. Again she spoke then walked off, her head held high, leaving Harvey to stare after her, nudging his hat higher on his head as if befuddled.

Roland smiled grimly. She'd obviously put the man in his place. Remembering the sting of her words, he could almost feel sorry for the poor brute.

Maybe she didn't need someone watching out for her, but that didn't prevent him from worrying about her or wanting to get to know her better. It seemed the woman was constantly on his mind. Question was, how could he achieve what looked to be more impossible with each passing day?

eight

Angel clutched the bed frame in a death grip. It shook like what she imagined it would feel going through an earthquake or hurricane. The railcar walls vibrated with a metallic clunking noise as if they might suddenly disintegrate in a strong wind.

She didn't remember this awful feeling of being about to take her last breath on the train she took a week ago, though the accommodations were nicer in Roland's private car and the dining compartment. Angel could hardly believe she'd lived on a train like this as a child. The carnival was much different than she'd once imagined, and except for the present situation with the fear that at any moment she might be shaken apart, she'd found a sense of harmony she'd never known at her aunt's home. The carnies she'd met so far were all wonderful, making her feel as if she belonged. None of them ever belittled a remark she made, which helped her to relax and feel freer to join in their conversations.

"You'll get used to it," her cabin mate said from the cot above. "What's really bad is traveling this way when your head feels like it's splitting wide open."

Angel could imagine this kind of travel giving her a headache.

"I heard you've been asking about your mother. Any luck with that?"

"No." Angel gave a weary sigh. "No one remembers her."

"Mind me asking why you're so intent on finding her, especially since you don't remember her?" Cassie paused as Angel struggled. "If you'd rather not say, or if you tell me to mind my own business, I'll understand."

It was actually nice to have someone in whom to confide, a benefit she'd never shared with her waspish cousins. She'd been able to speak with Nettie only between her friend's chores. Strange how Angel's aunt lamented the difficulty of surviving the Depression but kept Nettie on, though she never did pay the woman her worth. Keeping up appearances was paramount to Aunt Genevieve.

Angel squashed further bitter thoughts.

"I never felt like I belonged at my aunt's. I. . .I suppose if I ever do find my mother, there's a strong possibility she might not wish to see me. But I'm willing to take the risk." The more she thought about it, taking into account the behavior of her aunt and cousins, she wouldn't put it past them to lie about the cause of Lila's disappearance.

Cassie's head suddenly popped down as she hung over the cot, startling Angel into jumping back a little. Her new friend gave a goofy smile. How she could balance herself in an oversize tin can that felt as if it might rattle apart at any moment, Angel couldn't begin to imagine.

"Don't you get dizzy like that?"

"I'm an acrobat; it's my nature. When I was little, I thought I'd be a tightrope walker. But I prefer to do my daredevil stunts on things in motion—like my horses. Rattling train cars that zoom into the night work, too."

Angel grinned with admiration. If she tried doing what Cassie did, she would probably get herself killed.

"So if you find her, what then? Will you pretend like nothing's happened and ask her back into your life as a permanent fixture?"

"I suppose a lot depends on her. How you don't get sick to your stomach hanging like an opossum is beyond me."

"I'm tough." Cassie grinned. "Besides, I need the practice for my new act." She initiated a swift flip, holding to the edge of her bed while throwing her legs behind her and landing on the train floor, then threw her arms out with panache. "Ta-dah!"

Cassie's landing hadn't been solid, but Angel clapped, chuckling in awed disbelief. "Then you're going through with it?"

A determined look crossed her friend's pretty features. "Maybe if I show Papa I'm not a child anymore, he won't be so dead set against me seeing who I would like."

"Chester doesn't seem happy about the act either."

Cassie sighed. "Only because he doesn't think I'm ready. He has faith in me. That's one of the things I love about him." Her face grew rosy, and she quickly sank beside Angel on her cot. "What about you and Roland? I noticed you two haven't been getting along well lately."

"I wish people would stop pairing us off," Angel mumbled. "There's a lot you don't know about him. Things about his family. . ." She remembered her promise to keep his identity secret just in time. "They're not so nice."

"Well, I suppose if Chester let that stop him, we would never have gotten together. Not that we're together exactly," she added with haste.

"Cassie, it's okay. I won't tell. It's obvious you two are close."

Cassie sighed and nodded. "He wants to marry me."

"Cassie!"

"I told him no."

Angel thought back. "At the tent when Roland and I got there—"

"We were discussing it, yes. I can't go against Papa's wishes, but at the same time I don't want to live without Chester."

"Wouldn't Mahoney be upset if you two married?"

She scowled. "We can't live the entirety of our lives to suit our boss. I tried that, and I'm sick of it. After what Germaine did, running off with Lionel just because Mahoney didn't want them to marry. . . Truth is, I think he liked her. But Chester and I don't plan to leave the carnival, not that it matters. Not if I can't get Papa to change his mind."

"Doesn't it, um, bother you, how he takes care of his fleas?"

Cassie laughed, sounding relieved to change the subject. "I didn't like it one bit at first, let me tell you. But he's said it's safe; it's not like he could get a disease, since they aren't the type to bite animals." She shrugged. "I think when you love someone you just have to learn to take the fleas with the flowers." She grinned at her joke. "No one's perfect, Angel. You find that out pretty fast when working at a joint like this. Every man has his flaws or idiosyncrasies that you wish like everything you could change—and I'll bet the guys feel the same about us women. But if you love a person enough, you don't mind dealing with the problems or even ignoring them. Because there's so much more to appreciate. I love his laugh, the way he always tries to make others laugh, the way his eyes crinkle at the corners and. . ." She caught herself, embarrassed. "I just love being with him. And if living without a certain man is more difficult than living with him, imperfections and all, I think that's a basis for true love."

Cassie's words brought Roland to mind, which confused her. She didn't have feelings for him, and certainly, if she did, they would never include love. Still, she considered his main flaw: his mobster family. He couldn't change his origins, but he tried to change his future; she admired his perseverance in what she imagined couldn't be an easy challenge to undertake.

The train took a sudden sharp bend, throwing the girls against each other, and Angel again concentrated on striving to remain in one piece.

"Not to worry," Cassie assured her. "Won't be much longer. We should reach New Milford soon."

"I am so relieved to hear it!"

The girls looked at one another then giggled, and their conversation took on other directions as the train sped them to their destination.

❧

"How long did you say till we get there?" Roland didn't want to sound like a coward, but having never ridden in anything but his family's private car, he was getting a lesson in roughing it he would long remember. No one, but no one from the old life would imagine him in such a place. The thought pleased him.

With a maddening grin Chester eyed Roland's white-knuckled grip on the bedpost. "Track usually isn't so bad. Must have run into some rough. Winds are pretty high."

"You can say that again."

The train made another sharp rocking motion.

After endless minutes Roland heard the warning whistles and felt the train's momentum begin to slow.

"Don't look so smug yet. Now is where the fun really begins," Chester observed from where he sat on the floor, his back against the wall. "Once we pull in, we gotta get everything up and ready for tonight. Hope you got a good rest, 'cause you're gonna need it."

At Chester's amused grin, Roland shot his new—and at the moment, questionable—friend a dirty look. Rest? The man had to be pulling his leg. The travel had been about as restful as racing pell-mell across New York City in a car with bad springs while being chased, like when Roland was a boy and his bodyguard grew a little too careless flirting with the lady friend of a dangerous mobster who happened to be one of Grandfather's worst enemies. After that incident, the bodyguard disappeared. Roland imagined his new locale was the bottom of the Hudson River.

Even riding on a train with a conductor who seemed to prefer the idea of flying by airplane to traveling by land and tried to push his locomotive to the limits of the airborne daredevils couldn't compare with the fear of that summer day. Living as a Piccoli, Roland had lost track of the times he'd been certain his life would end. Despite the hardship, he felt doubly thankful he had followed Angel what seemed longer than a mere week ago. He preferred living in this atmosphere, a world apart from his wealthy and dangerous roots. The carnies treated him with suspicion at first—he was a novice at menial labor and hadn't had an easy time of gaining their trust, something he still worked at—but at least they hadn't questioned him about his past, and for that, Roland was grateful.

Exiting the train, his legs still shaky, he noticed the glow of dawn filled the sky. The train had pulled off onto a sidetrack, away from the junction and out in the wilds, as before.

The roustabouts immediately began setting up the rides, and the meal tent was erected on the other side of the lot, breakfast administered rapidly. Afterward, with no idea what was expected of him, he searched out Mama Philena. She handed him a bucket of paste and a long-handled brush. "I'll take care of the animals. You go into town and hang flyers. On the sides of buildings, anywhere they'll fit."

He remained still when she turned to go. "Aren't you forgetting something?" He lifted the items he held in emphasis when she only stared. "The flyers?"

"Oh, I'm not forgetting anything, dearie. It's a two-man job. Your partner has them. Waiting over there for you, by Samson's railcar. Best hurry. It's a long walk into town."

Mama turned away, chuckling most wickedly, her shiny purple shirt seeming to echo her devious behavior, crackling with laughter at him as it rustled with her swift movements. He harbored no doubt about the identity of his partner. When he reached Angel waiting near the train, he went into surrender before she could pose an attack.

"I promise I had no part in this. If you want me to find someone else to help me, I will."

A grin, both amused and exasperated, lifted her mouth. "Oh don't be silly, Roland. I'm not mad. They do seem determined to put us together though, don't they? It's actually quite strange, when you consider it, since

Mahoney's number one rule for his carnival seems to be to discourage close rapport between male and female carnies." She shrugged in an offhand manner, further baffling him. "I don't mind working with you. Are you ready?"

Her eyes sparkled, as if she anticipated the outing.

Would he ever figure her out?

The walk to town was a few miles, but time seemed to pass quickly now that Angel had let down her guard and conversed on friendly terms. They talked of everything: the carnival; their experiences with it; the weather, sunny and clear. But they avoided the subject of their lives as if by unspoken agreement. Roland was almost sorry when they arrived in town, a pretty little community with the usual Victorian-style houses and stores, with a strip of short grass and blooming trees running along its center.

They chose a building with old, peeling posters as their first mark. While Angel held the carnival flyer against the wood, Roland executed a few swipes of paste over the paper with the brush until it rested flat against the building. Angel let out a little squeal when the bristles whisked over her hand.

"Sorry. This is my first experience doing this sort of thing."

"That's okay." She rubbed the back of her sticky hand on a leg of her denim trousers. "I imagine, with the life you've led, you're not accustomed to manual labor of any. . .regular sort."

Her words were cautious, her manner intent, and he recognized her desire to know more.

"You really don't want to know, Angel."

"Did you. . ." Her teeth pulled at her lip. "Did you kill anyone?"

Why did that always seem to be the first question the ladies asked? "No. But if I'd stuck around, my grandfather would have put me in a position to do so. He made that very clear at our last meeting."

She gave an abrupt nod. "Okay, so I guess we should find

our next spot. Mama said fences or anywhere posters have been hanging and public buildings. They cleared it with those in charge, I would hope." She quickly moved away.

He followed her with brush and bucket. "I put that life behind me, Angel."

"I know."

"But it still scares you."

She hesitated. "Can you blame me? All I know about you Piccolis is what I read in the papers. And what I've heard from others."

"We're not all cut from the same cloth. A cousin doesn't approve of the family business either. He's the quiet type though. Doesn't have the nerve to stand up against his father."

"What about your fiancée? How does she feel about it?"

"My *what*?" Stunned, he stopped walking. Her face was rosier, and he wondered if the exertion of the walk or the nature of the question had caused it.

"The papers said—"

"The papers. The society pages, no doubt." Roland grimaced at the reporters' tendency to get facts incorrect and spin their own web of tales to sell their blasted papers. "Well, they got it wrong. I'm not engaged."

"But—"

"I was almost engaged, for two weeks. We were thrown together by our families. Both of us realized it wouldn't work. She loves someone else, and I don't love her. End of story."

"Sorry. I didn't mean to be so nosy."

The tension left his muscles. "It's all right. No harm done."

"My aunt wanted me to marry someone, too. It's part of why I ran."

Taken aback, this time by her unexpected confidence, he shot her another look. He felt encouraged that she had relaxed with him enough to talk about her past and on her own initiative.

"Hey, mister!"

They turned to see a freckle-faced youngster, his brown hair uncombed and sticking out in tufts, his pants worn in the knees and a little too long. He looked around nine years of age.

"Whatcha carryin' a pail and brush for?"

"We're part of the carnival about three miles down the road."

The boy's eyes sparkled in excitement. "In Sutter's Field?"

"I. . .don't know. It's a field, near the depot."

"Shouldn't you be in school?" Angel gently chided.

The boy scowled. "Aw, book learning's for sissies."

"I'm no sissy, and I read books." Roland thought the boy's arrogant attitude toward education was much like his brother's. "An education will always benefit your mind and will keep working for you as you grow older." He felt Angel's stare and wondered if he was being too hard on the youngster.

The boy shrugged. "Can't go anyhow. Not since things got so bad. Mama needs me at home while Pa looks for work and Rex, too. That's my brother. I'm Sam. I'm runnin' an errand for Mama now."

Roland felt remorseful for his stiff words. After living a privileged lifestyle when it came to assets, it was too easy to forget the nation suffered a depression. "I'm sorry, son."

"How long will the carnival be here?"

"A couple of weeks, I imagine." Roland glanced at Angel, who shrugged. The flyers didn't say. He looked back at the boy. "I hope things go better for your family. We need to hang the rest of these posters now."

"Okay."

The boy dogged their steps up the road. He talked a mile a minute, and Roland thought a career as a carnival barker might be a strong prospect for his future. Their small, self-appointed guide pointed out buildings, talked about their owners, whether he did or didn't like them, and expressed a strong desire to visit the carnival. Roland wondered if Sam was forgetting his errand.

Together he and Angel pasted another flyer to a building, and the boy watched, engrossed. He followed them as they completed two more. Once they finished, he grinned.

"I gotta go now." He moved toward the druggist's, next door to the wall where they had hung the poster.

"If you come to the carnival, look me up," Roland said before Sam could disappear. "I'm a caretaker of the animals. We even have a live elephant."

"No foolin'? An elephant? Hot diggety dog! Wait'll I tell Joey. And he thought finding that turtle was so great!" He rushed into the building, and Roland smiled, remembering his own boyhood excitement and curiosities.

If only the warm feeling could have lasted.

Roland's blood froze as he caught sight of a thickset man wearing a three-piece, pin-striped suit and fedora five buildings away, near a lamppost. He slipped the bucket handle over his wrist, took the brush leaning against the building, and grabbed Angel's arm with his free hand, turning her quickly with him in the opposite direction.

"Hey!" She looked at him in confusion but didn't try to break his grip.

"Just keep walking."

He kept his voice low but couldn't mask his alarm. Her eyes widened, and she started to look over her shoulder.

"Don't look, Angel."

Quickly she focused ahead. Once they reached the corner of the next building and darted around it, he peered around the side, then he pressed his back against the wall and closed his eyes in a dizzying mix of anxiety not to be found and relief to have escaped.

"I should have known the conductor might say something about my sudden disappearance," he muttered. "My grandfather has close ties with the company."

All color drained from her face. "Your f–family? H–here?"

"He was too far away to make out, but a man back there looked like one of Grandfather's associates." Roland doubted many citizens of New Milford wore such expensive suits or had the ox like build Giuseppe did. And Grandfather's men traveled in pairs, which meant Giuseppe's partner, Lorenzo, wasn't far. "We need to get back to the carnival. Now."

She gave a jerky nod, her eyes round with the same apprehension he felt.

"It's all right, Angel. He didn't see me. If we head around the back and circle the buildings, we should be safe. I won't let anyone hurt you." Again he clasped her arm, this time gently, his manner intense. He noticed her state of shock and gave her shoulder a shake to break her out of her daze.

"Are you with me?" He kept his tone calm but firm.

"Yes," she whispered.

He smiled to reassure her, though he felt just as anxious, and pulled her with him through the first phase of his plan. To his relief they found their way back to where they started, unobserved.

On the open road Roland felt like a sitting duck. He doubted Giuseppe would shoot; in all likelihood, his orders were to bring him back unharmed. But Giuseppe had no respect for women, those not connected with the family, and Roland dreaded the idea of him coming in contact with Angel, uncertain what the goon might do. The best-case scenario would be if he demanded she come with them; the worst- case. . .Roland didn't dare imagine the worst case.

Not once did he release his hold on Angel's arm, and he felt the tremors of fear that moved through her. She managed to keep up with his rapid gait but didn't say a word. Once the carnival tents came in sight, he felt her relax and heard her protracted sigh of relief.

"I'm really sorry about all this," he said grimly before they joined the others. He looked back at the road to make sure they weren't followed. "I guess you had the right idea all along about staying as far away from me as you could."

Instead of fleeing his company, as he was sure she would do once he released her, she whirled to face him, her eyes intense. "Are you in danger if he finds you?"

Shocked that she should care, it took him a moment to respond. "He probably only has orders to bring me home. But Angel. . ." He took a deep breath. "I told you once that you weren't in danger. With Giuseppe I can't make that promise. Of all the men my grandfather could have sent, he's the worst of the bunch."

She didn't ask him to explain, and he didn't care to.

"What will you do now?"

"I'll leave the carnival. I can't put anyone else in danger."

"But—where will you go? Won't you be in even more danger if you leave, since you said that here you can blend in and that your grandfather's men wouldn't be caught dead in a place like this?"

"I can't take that risk now."

She grabbed his arm, again startling him.

"You can't put yourself at risk either. You'll be easier to spot if you leave such a crowded place. And you said they could be ruthless, even to family."

"It's *my* family, Angel. I'm not going to let anyone here suffer because I had the luckless curse of being born a Piccoli."

"You can't leave," she insisted. "Talk to Mama; tell her about this. She'd be easier to talk to than Mahoney, and she *is* his mother. I'm sure she'd agree. And if you don't tell her, I will."

His mouth dropped open.

She nodded in emphasis. "She should know, Roland. She should know if there's a predator out there who might come to the carnival, in order to be prepared for whatever happens next. And she can tell her son if she feels there is a need."

He let out a harsh breath followed by a mild oath. "You're right. I'll tell her. Then I'll go."

"How? By train? They'll find you for sure. No, Roland. If you leave now, it could be the end of all you wanted. To break away from your family and what they stand for."

He looked at her curiously. "Why should you care? Ever since we met, all you've wanted is for me to steer clear of you. Now that opportunity has arrived, and you want me to stay? Why?"

She blinked, taken off guard, her gaze dropping to the ground. She seemed to realize she still held his arm and released it, her manner almost shy. "I. . .don't know." She looked up again, determined. "Yes, I do. I don't want to see you get hurt either. So I guess now the shoe's back on the other foot."

"You, playing my guardian angel?" he asked softly, still trying to grasp the sudden switch in her feelings.

"Yeah." She grinned. "If you want to call it that. Would you like me to go with you to talk to Mama?"

He cocked his brow. "Don't trust me to stick around?" Such words, delivered to Angel of all people, seemed incredible. He couldn't understand her change of heart. Thrown into the mix of danger, she hadn't pushed him away or fled.

"I just thought you might like some support."

Again she surprised him, and he realized he wanted her beside him more than anything. He managed a faint grin. "Yeah, I would."

For the time being he would honor her wishes. But their near escape made him realize that in order to do what he needed and become his own man while severing family ties, he would have to find a place where no one could locate him.

He withheld a groan, wondering if such an asylum existed anywhere on the planet.

nine

Angel watched Mama Philena slowly nod, her eyes steady, not one change in her stolid expression as Roland finished informing her of the facts.

"You don't seem all that surprised." He regarded her with disbelief.

"With what? That you're a Piccoli? Or that your grandfather sent his men to hunt you down?"

"Either. Both." Huffing a confused breath, lifting his hands, he shook his head in bewilderment.

"I knew you were hiding something the moment I saw you. Remember"—she smiled and pointed to her temple—"I can read a person well. That said, I think you should stay."

"That's what I told him," Angel said, relieved, and Mama turned her smile on her.

"Maybe I didn't make clear to you the dangers," Roland explained patiently. "If I stay, my presence at your carnival could put everyone at risk."

"Maybe you don't understand the power of God," Mama responded just as tolerantly. "He brought you here; I'm sure of it now. And whatever His reasons, He can handle the situation."

Both Angel and Roland stared, speechless.

Mama chuckled. "Guess you two don't know much about Him, from the looks on your faces. That, too, can change." Her smile was secretive, the twinkle in her eyes somehow comforting.

"I have a friend, Nettie," Angel said. "She feels the same way you do and spoke to me about the Bible, though I never

nderstood half of what she said. But she said the same
ing—that I should trust God to work things out. That
e always would."

Mama nodded. "It takes experience sometimes to under-
and the root of things people tell you. But once you've seen
e Almighty at work—and by the way, He doesn't just have
at name as an exaggerated hook to draw in the crowds, like
me performers here do—you'll know what I say is genuine."

Roland cleared his throat. "I should talk this over with
Mahoney and Pearson. Neither of you seem to understand
e dangers. These are trained men. With guns. And with-
ut scruples."

"No reason to talk to the boys." Mama, for the first time
nce Angel met her, looked sheepish. "This is the time for
onfessions? Well, all right, I have one, too. The carnival is
ine. I own it."

The resulting silence came brief but so thick Angel felt
rapped inside it.

"My husband left it to me," Mama continued, "but I let
y son run things. It gave his life direction again. After his
ife died, so young, he needed something to set his mind
, and I'm no good with figures and such, so it was the
erfect arrangement. His partner is my nephew—it's all a
amily affair." She grinned. "I don't broadcast that I'm the
ue owner—only those few carnies who've been with us
e longest know—but I have controlling interest and all
nportant decisions go through me first. So, since this is my
arnival, I say you stay. Now. . ."

She clapped her hands and stood, a sign that the urgent
eeting Roland had requested was over. "We have work to
o if we're going to have things up and running by tonight.
Get busy. Roland, go help the other men raise the tents.
ngel, you can help me."

Angel and Roland stared at each other. Clearly he was

also at a loss at being so quickly reassured, dismissed, an
assigned orders.

"Well, what are you waiting for?" Mama asked Roland
"The tents aren't going to erect themselves."

"Talk to you later?" He posed his soft question to Ange
and she nodded. He smiled. "All right then. Ladies." H
tipped his hat to them both and left.

Angel watched him go.

Mama chuckled from behind, and Angel heard her mut
ter "Oh no. Not a thing going on there at all!"

Feeling heat flush her cheeks, Angel didn't dare face Mama

Over the next few hours Angel found out what a stron
support the woman was to the carnival. No job was beneat]
her. If she had the stamina, she did it, and Angel helpec
They aided carnies in setting up the insides of their tents
fed the animals, scrubbed cutlery and dishes when Milli
complained of feeling poorly, hoisted poles through meta
rungs secured at the ends of banners to fly high overhead, se
up tables and booths, shoveled in dirt to pack and flatten
dangerous pit that was part of the midway where a custome
might fall—and when Angel was sure nothing was left to b
done, Mama surprised her and took her on another roun
of odd and sundry chores. Angel was speechless with aw
at Mama's tenacity mixed with a strength she never woul
have suspected in a petite, reed-thin woman in her sixties.

With her cheeks sore from blowing air into balloon
for one of the game booths, Angel took a cooling drink o
cream soda and observed how each of the carnies treate
Mama with respect. Even those who wanted little to d
with anyone else gave Mama a listening ear.

The afternoon's labor helped Angel forget the morning
fright. Having blown up the last of the colorful balloons an
handed them to Fletcher, the agent for that booth, who pinne
them to a board where darts would be thrown by paying cus

tomers, Angel found her hands suddenly unoccupied. Mama stood a short distance away, giving advice to one of the carnies who'd sought her out. And with irritating ease Angel's thoughts returned to her confusion over Roland.

He wasn't the only one flummoxed by her change of heart. She couldn't understand either what led to her desperation for him to stay. But when she suddenly ran smack into the dangers he had daily lived and realized he was ready to sacrifice all his hopes, perhaps even his life, to protect her and everyone there, the thought of something terrible happening to him made her blood run cold. She'd heard that expression before, but she'd never understood it until she shivered from the chill that raised gooseflesh on her skin when he told her he would leave and she'd never see him again.

At that bizarre moment his words she had long wished to hear became the dread she hoped never to face. She didn't want him to go; she wanted him to stay, though she restrained from delving too far into the reasons why.

Could life get any more insanely complicated?

"Finished with the balloons?" Mama approached, her face flushed rosy from work and sun. "You'd best get to Millie's tent and help with the food. With that stomach upset of hers, you might need to take over."

Angel hid a wince. She hoped that watching the cook through the past week would be enough to manage on her own. After one trial effort of Angel's work, Millie never asked her to prepare food again, except for the toast, which Angel did well.

"I enjoyed working with you today, Mama." Much more than sitting on a stool selling tickets. "It was fascinating to see how everything is done from all angles and be able to help those who needed it."

Mama tilted her head to the side. "I think you have a servant's heart, Angel. It's what I love most about my carnival, helping those who need a hand."

"We finished sooner than I expected. I understood it would take most of the day."

"Oh, there's still plenty of work to be done. Next I'll be headed to the Tent of Wonders to see if anyone needs a hand there. Don't like calling them freaks."

Angel's heart stopped beating. "Can I come with you? I'm really not a good cook." She hoped her confession would trigger the invitation she had long desired.

"Any specific reason you want to visit there?" Mama's expression grew guarded. "Even though Tucker thinks he owns them and displays them like cattle for money, I'm protective of all my family. They're people with souls, not creatures to be constantly gawked at. They get enough of that when the carnival is open to the public."

Angel had asked Cassie and other longtime workers about her mother but had lost hope of anyone knowing her on her fourth day there. She realized she'd never told Mama, since she rarely spent time in her company. "My mother was one of those so-called freaks." She winced at the word, also not liking it. "A bearded lady named Lila. I'm hoping one day to find her." The words, once so hard to say, now spilled off her tongue.

Mama stood frozen, but Angel was growing accustomed to this kind of reaction. Shock was better than the slight repulsion or blatant curiosity she'd also witnessed from those few carnies she'd told, whose gazes then intently scoured her jaw, as if searching for some sign of the imperfection her mother suffered.

"Is that a fact?" Mama breathed softly. "Well now, who would've guessed. . . ?"

"I've asked around but haven't had any luck. I'm still hoping to find someone who knew her or of her, maybe even worked where she did, since I discovered a lot of carnies here have come from other places."

"Yes. I've hired a number of performers who come from shows like mine." Mama stared at Angel as if making a decision. "All right then. Come with me. Jezebel," she said in passing to a young carny, "help Millie with supper. Let me know if she's feeling worse."

"Sure will, Aunt Philena." She nodded in curiosity to Angel before she took off running, her long black braids bouncing as she went.

"Jezzie is my nephew's daughter," Mama explained as they walked, and she threw Angel a sidelong smile. "Like I said, we're all one big family here. Those not by blood grafted in by the unique talents each has to offer."

Angel sucked in a nervous breath as Mama swept through the tent, then she followed. Seven people worked inside, one man looking less than pleased to see the newcomers.

"Everything's taken care of." A gruff-looking character with the stump of a cigar sticking out of his pudgy lips, he gave Angel the willies. "Don't need your services today."

"Speak for yourself, Tucker." A high girlish voice that Angel recognized came from her right. She watched Posey move eagerly forward and gave the woman a genuine smile, happy to see her again.

"Hi, Posey. How are plans for the wedding coming along?"

Mama looked from one to the other in surprise. "You two know each other?"

"You could say we ran into each other—almost," Angel joked, and Posey laughed.

"I'm having trouble with my gown." She held up her short, thick fingers. "Can't hold a flimsy needle well, but I'm managing."

"I could help." Angel felt all eyes on her and blushed. "I'm somewhat handy with a needle. I've sewn my own dresses and my cousins', too."

"That would be swell!" Posey fairly bubbled. "Maybe you

could help Rita and Rosa out, too—that is, if you wouldn't mind?"

"It's what I came for. To help." She glanced at Mama, and the woman smiled and nodded.

"Come along then, and meet the rest of the bunch." Posey took Angel's hand, pulling her toward the back of the large tent. "You've seen Jim at the cook tent, I'm sure." Angel smiled in greeting toward the giant, who tipped his hat and inclined his head in polite acknowledgment. "And that's Gunter." She motioned to a brown-skinned man covered in tattoos and piercings; even his eyelids had pictures on them. At her uncertain nod, he inclined his head slowly, unsmiling, his black eyes wary. "And you've met my darling prince."

"Hullo again." Darrin waved a casual, two-fingered salute from his brow.

"And this is Rita and Rosa."

Two pretty young women with bright green eyes and short black curls sat on chairs pressed close to each other. Angel blinked, realizing the women were joined at the shoulders.

"I'm Rita." The one on Angel's left offered her right hand.

"And I'm Rosa." She offered her left.

Angel shook each hand in turn, trying not to stare at the area that made them different.

"They're not seamstresses either," Posey explained. "And they've run into a problem for tonight's show."

"We tore our costume. See?" Rita sadly displayed a long tear in the shimmering crimson skirt.

"Speak for yourself, sister. If you'd not been so quick to move. . ."

"And if you'd not been so slothful to stay. . ."

"We would not be in this predicament," they finished together.

Posey tugged at Angel's skirt and grinned when she

ooked her way. "They're like this all the time. Don't pay any attention."

Angel smiled at Posey then directed her nervous gaze to the wins. "If you, um, have a needle and thread, I can sew it up."

"Would you?" Rita asked. "You're an angel!"

At that both Angel and Posey laughed, and Angel's tension drained away.

"Did I say something funny?" Rita looked at Rosa, who shrugged her free shoulder.

"Ladies, this *is* Angel," Posey explained. "The girl I told you about."

"Ooo—the one who came here with that handsome young man," Rosa exclaimed.

Angel didn't bother to correct her, weary of the undertaking.

"I hear you're looking for your mother," Rita said, enlightenment coming into her eyes. "Lila."

Angel's heartbeat quickened. "You know her?"

"Sorry, no."

"We joined Mahoney's carnival a little over a year ago."

"But another carny who once worked with us mentioned Bruce, a strongman who married a bearded lady named Lila, from another carnival. He mentioned she had a little girl. I'm guessing that was you."

Angel nodded, a twinge in her heart. "Do you know where I can find him? The other carny?"

Both girls shook their heads. "No, sorry," Rita said, "Abe left about the time we joined up."

Angel nodded and managed a smile, trying not to allow yet another sting of disappointment to wound her. If Abe knew them and he once worked here, there might be others who also did.

With quiet thanks, accepting the needle, thread, and a stool that Darrin brought her, Angel set to work, skillfully mending the rip. As the three women talked, she found herself easily entering into their conversation. She hadn't known how she would react upon meeting those who worked inside this tent. After having her desire met, at first she felt awkward, not wanting to be rude, but the curiosity of human nature caused her eyes to stray more than once to the differences that set them apart. But as the minutes passed, she relaxed, perhaps not able to ignore their oddities, as she would have wished, but able to accept these girls, just as she accepted and enjoyed their company. How strange that on such short acquaintance she felt closer to them than she'd ever felt with her cousins.

She would have liked to stay and chat longer, but Mama, having finished treating a boil on Gunter's leg, announced to Angel they had more work to do.

"It was a pleasure meeting all of you," Angel said to the group then turned her attention to the twins and Posey. "I'd love to be able to visit with you again."

"Yes. . ."

"We'd like that. . . . That is, if. . ."

Both girls turned nervous glances toward their manager. Tucker glared at the twins, Angel, and Posey, his arms crossed over his thickset chest.

"Why, I think that would be a lovely idea, Angel." Mama gave Tucker her own baleful stare. "They usually prefer to take their meals here, or outside at the back of the tent on nice days, except for Jim. So you can deliver them in my place."

Angel smiled her gratitude, ignoring Tucker. It was Mama's carnival after all.

"Thanks again, Angel, the dress looks wonderful—"

"Better than when we got it."

"What do you mean, 'we'? I'm the one who picked it out. . . ."

As the two sisters quietly bickered, Angel turned her

attention to Posey. "Give me your gown, and I'll see what I can do."

"Oh, would you?" Posey practically squealed, clasping her hands beneath her chin. "Thank you, thank you, thank you! I'll be back in a flash." She whirled around and sped to a curtained area of the tent.

"You heard Mama!" Tucker bellowed. "There's work to be done here."

"Oh, I think a few minutes more for Posey to fetch her gown won't hurt anything," Mama answered sweetly.

Angel looked at the two, discerning the friction that seethed between them.

Minutes later, once Angel had Posey's gown in hand and they had left the tent, Mama addressed the matter of Tucker. "That man is as rough as sandpaper," she groused. "But with a good deal of prayer—and believe me, I've spent time on my knees for him, too—I suppose God can even take care of a man like Tucker and smooth out the grainy bits."

Angel thought a moment. "If I pray, do you think God might help me find my mother?"

Her hopeful words melted the stern look off Mama's features. "It's that important to you?"

"Yes. I—I never knew her." She didn't bother telling her she thought she was dead up until a few weeks before.

"Well, child. God can mend anything. With a little prayer. And sometimes it might take a lot, as in the case of Tucker." Mama slyly winked.

Angel thought about Mama's words all the rest of the afternoon and on through the evening as she sold tickets outside the tent with Cassie's act. Mama and Nettie thought a lot alike. Two people of different race, background, culture, and personality—but both retained the same strong beliefs in God and His power, and both were excited about it, making Angel wonder. She had attended Sunday morning services with Aunt Genevieve and her cousins but had never really listened to the elderly minister, whose quiet voice droned on and on, often making her sleepy or causing her mind to wander in countless directions.

"Hello!" a bright voice snapped Angel out of her musings. She counted change back into a customer's hand for the two ten-cent tickets he purchased and turned to the girl who hailed her.

"Jezebel?" Angel expressed surprise to see the girl, perhaps three years younger than herself.

"I was asked to take over your spot for a while."

"Take over?" Angel put the dollar into the strongbox. "Why?"

"Because I asked her to," a deep voice suddenly said from nearby, startling Angel and setting her pulse to pounding.

"Roland?"

"Cassie wants you to see her act."

She saw now that Chester stood behind him, his face tense. "I'm going in there and try to talk her out of it. Fool girl'll break her neck just to prove a point."

He hurried toward the tent, and Angel looked at Roland. "The new stunt?" she whispered.

He nodded, and quickly she joined him. Chester's words fed Angel's fear; he seemed to know Cassie better than anyone, and if he was worried. . .

Angel offered a silent prayer for her stubborn friend, hoping she formed her words right, though she wasn't on her knees, hoping God would hear her petition, hoping above all else that Cassie would be protected from danger.

ten

Inside the huge tent, spectators sat on benches in graduated levels and watched the center ring with the thrill of excitement. Only Angel and Roland viewed the unfolding events with absolute dread.

Cassie's mother stood with one foot atop each of two Andalusians running side by side, while a man in a matching flashy silver and gold costume stood in the center and held a prod. Roland scanned the right side of the tent and found the person they sought.

"There she is," he said to Angel, nodding to the closed-off area.

Beyond the gap of hanging tapestries, Roland spotted Chester, red in the face, looking as if he was giving his girl an earful. Cassie's expression was just as obstinate. Roland noticed her father catch sight of them as he turned in time with the horses then did a quick double take. But he continued with the act while his wife switched to one stallion and did a handstand amid a burst of applause. Once she'd traveled the ring and lowered herself to both feet again, in one move jumping down to straddle the horse and bring it to a slow stop, her husband announced a short intermission before the next act, saying his wife would answer any questions. She looked at him oddly, and Roland assumed this wasn't part of their show. But with an inviting smile she sat sideways on her horse and pointed to an eager youngster with his hand raised.

Her husband moved behind her to where Cassie now sat mounted while Chester firmly held the horse's bridle and looked up at her. By their stiff features, nothing had changed.

Her father entered the fray. His displeasure at seeing Chester near his daughter soon turned toward Cassie as both men wore equal expressions of disapproval. Cassie's jaw remained set. She shook her blond ringlets tersely and proceeded, urging the horse to the ring and cutting off further questions from the audience to her mother.

Roland felt Angel's hands circle the muscle of his arm.

"She's really going to do it," she whispered in fear, and Roland grimly surmised the same thing. "Dear God, protect her." He barely heard the words leave her lips.

Cassie's mother rode out of the ring, clearly unaware of the tension or her daughter's decision as she dismounted and started another lively record on the phonograph. Chester and her father stood side by side with hands clenched on the wooden bar that separated the ring from spectators, their looks of anxious worry matched, while Cassie blithely waved to the crowd and performed her first act. Her movements were graceful, limber as she brought herself to stand atop the cantering horse, as nimble as its rider. Steps and movements led one into another, so fluidly she executed what looked like an acrobatic ballet as she took turns moving to sit and stand atop the horse.

Roland was impressed.

"She's really very good," Angel related his thoughts in awe. Her grip on his arm relaxed.

Cassie again stood straight on one leg and toed her foot before her. Her mother had joined her husband, clearly curious why he left the ring. He spoke, and she swung around as if to rush forward and try to stop Cassie. Her husband's hand on her arm stopped her.

Roland could almost tell how the young bareback rider judged her timing by the expression on her face, her smile not as bright, her features fixed as she stood, arms to the sides, and seemed to count.

"I can't watch." Angel turned her head into his shoulder. The feel of her nestled there brought a strong surge of warmth through his blood along with a desire to console. He cupped his hand to her head, her hair like silk beneath his touch.

Roland held his breath, also certain they would soon be carrying Cassie's broken body from the ring. A quick glance toward Chester showed his face, now pale, his eyes wide and intent on the woman he loved. Not sure he fully believed in the intervening power of God, Roland found himself muttering the same prayer Angel had for the stubborn girl's protection and for the trick to work.

Cassie suddenly vaulted into the air, bringing her legs up over her head in a graceful backward somersault. Her white and silver-sequined costume shimmered from the lights of many lanterns. In one breathless, heart-stopping moment it looked as if she might miss. . . .

The crowd gasped, echoing Roland's swift intake of breath.

She landed, finding solid footing near the back of the horse, and raised her arms high, her smile dazzling in her triumph.

The audience exploded with applause, many jumping to their feet. Chester whooped and threw his hat high. Her mother seemed to collapse against her husband, whose slow smile expressed grudging admiration for his daughter.

"She did it." Angel's words trembled, as if she might cry. "Oh Roland, she really did it!" She threw both her arms around his neck, hugging him fiercely.

Her soft warmth unexpectedly pressed against him knocked Roland's mental capabilities awry and didn't do much for his spiraling emotions either. He couldn't think of an answer to give, his tongue suddenly thick; if he did try to talk, he feared it would come out as gibberish.

She seemed to realize what she was doing and drew away, sending him a demure, embarrassed glance from beneath her lashes before turning her attention to the ring again.

"She truly is a wonder."

Roland didn't want to talk or think about Cassie or the performance. He would rather focus on the woman who'd just held him so tightly, maybe even take her somewhere quiet and give in to his desire to discuss a potential relationship—though what he really wished to do, he realized in the moment she embraced him, was kiss her.

No opportunity presented itself for further conversation or a second daring demonstration on his part, for as Roland looked past the ring to the spectators, he caught sight of an oxlike man in a pin-striped suit, a smaller man dressed in a similar manner beside him. Neither seemed interested in the performance, both intently scanning the crowds.

"Angel," he said just loudly enough so she could hear above the frenzied clapping. "I want you to walk away from me now, turn around, and leave the tent."

"What? Why?" Instead of doing as he asked, she looked to where his gaze was fixed. She gasped, and he knew the moment she realized new danger, as she again grabbed both his arm and his hand, intent on pulling him with her.

&

"It's them, isn't it? You have to get out of here, too!" Whether it was Cassie's bold defiance to do what no one expected she could, or her earlier thoughts of this man that spurred Angel's own courage, she didn't know or care. But she wasn't about to flee two gangsters while leaving Roland to their doubtful mercy. "Come on!" She persistently tugged, refusing to let him go. He had no choice but to follow or bring attention their way by attempting to break contact.

"Angel, this is crazy," he muttered once she pulled him out of the tent.

"No crazier than you thinking you have to become a sacrifice for your family's sins! Let's tell Mama they're here. She'll know what to do."

He hesitated, and she thought she might have to pull him bodily down the midway. He was lean but hard and muscular, she'd learned during her spontaneous embrace, while she was slight of build but determined. "They might step outside any second. Do you really want to stand here and argue about this and risk them finding both of us?"

Her words snapped Roland out of his indecision. Grimly he nodded, and they hurried down the midway. They found Mama at Jabar's act and filled her in on the news.

"I see." Her usually merry eyes became grim. "Well then, we should teach those two that their type isn't welcome here. Jabar. . ." She turned to the boy who sat atop his elephant. "I think Jenny would like a walk."

He grinned and nodded.

Angel and Roland watched curiously.

"We'll make one stop at Corinthos's tent. I think that should be enough of a welcome committee, don't you?" Her smile was sly.

Angel couldn't help but grin. The Snake Man wore his pet boas around his shoulders, chest, and arms. Every time she saw him thus embellished, it gave her the jitters.

Roland caught on with a slow smile. "Come to think of it, I seem to remember Giuseppe has a fear of reptiles."

"Good. You two stay out of sight. No use letting them know you're here. Jenny and the snakes are just an. . .added precaution?" Mama smiled, though it didn't reach her eyes.

Once she left with Jabar and Jenny, Roland looked at Angel. "I've got to see this."

"You're not leaving me behind!" She grabbed his arm again, rather beginning to like the connection.

"No, I didn't think so. Let's go then. We can watch from a distance."

They followed, taking note of how quickly Corinthos agreed to Mama's request. He informed his audience he would return soon. Some of the crowd followed the foursome down the midway, curious to see an elephant with a small Arab boy in a turban perched atop, a silver-haired wraith of a woman in a sky blue satin dress leading the way like an aged warrior princess, and a tall, brawny man wrapped in snakes walking alongside the elephant.

Roland suddenly tensed beneath Angel's hold and brought his hand across her chest to grab her shoulder in warning, moving with her to a shielding tent. She caught sight of the gangsters, who stood out in the crowd. Their manner of doing business also garnered attention. The huge one had his meaty fist bunched around the shirt of one of the carnies, smaller by half, as he threatened him with his raised fist.

Mama calmly walked up to the men. "I don't allow any violence at my carnival." Her voice came out quiet, authoritative, and Angel admired her daring.

"Is that a fact? So, maybe we won't have to knock any heads together," the smaller man said. "Just tell us where to find Roland Piccoli."

Angel's shoulders stiffened at hearing his name, and she tightened her hold around his arm, afraid he might actually step forward and reveal himself if things grew too heated. His absentminded pats to her hand did little to comfort.

"Piccoli. . .Piccoli. . .Corinthos, you know anyone by the name of Piccoli?"

The Snake Man stepped out from beyond the elephant and into sudden view of the pair. The two gangsters jumped back, clearly disturbed at the sight of the spotted reptile that slowly moved in layers of coils around the man. Angel felt the quiver of Roland's chest as he quietly chuckled.

"No, Mama," Corinthos replied in an articulated accent, almost British like Blackie's but not quite that, either. His deep voice sounded both distinguished and sinister. His steady eyes settled on the gangsters. Even without the snakes, the dark-skinned man stood tall, formidable, and well muscled.

"Look here, we don't want no trouble," the bigger of the two gangsters said, his wide eyes never leaving the snakes.

"But we'll give it, if that's what it takes." The smaller man reached into his suit coat for what was undoubtedly a gun, and Angel saw the flash of metal. Roland hissed between his teeth, taking a quick step forward. Angel held his arm in a death grip, keeping him back.

"Jenny," Mama said quickly, pointing to the gangster, "find the peanut!"

Jenny's trunk eagerly swept up the man's shirtfront, and he let out a terrified howl. "Get that thing off me!" Jenny's trunk found his hand with the gun. As if realizing danger, she squeezed around his wrist. The man let out a yelp of pain, his weapon falling to the ground.

"Jenny, release." The elephant dropped her trunk away at Jabar's order. The man clutched his wrist. Jabar moved Jenny forward a step, and her foot, the size of a small tree trunk, stepped squarely on the weapon.

"You *gentlemen*"—Mama made the reference dryly—"will now leave my carnival. I don't take kindly to threats, and neither does my family. Should you decide to ignore my warning and return, I'll be sure to have Corinthos here aid you."

The Snake Man delivered a smile full of straight ivory teeth, and the manner in which he studied the gangsters was threatening, as if he was eager for the opportunity to meet them again. Angel knew it was all for show and what he, as a performer, did best. Corinthos was really most genial, even courteous, when Angel talked to him on occasion while serving him breakfast. But she shivered at the menacing picture he now presented.

"Get out." Mama's words were severe. "And don't come back. Corinthos will escort you to the entrance."

The Snake Man stepped in their direction. The two gangsters retreated awkwardly, almost stumbling over each other. "Come on, Giuseppe. That playboy wouldn't be caught dead in a dive like this. Don't know why you were thinking he might. Let's get outta here." Turning tail, they hurried away.

"Follow them," Mama told Corinthos.

He swept his head and shoulders down in a slight, gracious bow. "My pleasure, Mama."

The crowd who had followed and others who gathered burst into applause, obviously thinking it all an act for their entertainment. Mama didn't correct them. "Thank you, one and all!" She beamed. "There's plenty more to see and do. We appreciate your business. Be sure and come again—and tell your friends."

Once the crowd dispersed, Mama turned to the elephant. "Good girl, Jenny." She patted her above the trunk near her docile brown eyes. "You deserve a whole sack full of peanuts for that maneuver. Jabar, tell Simmons I said Jenny is to have a special treat."

"Yes, Mama!" The boy guided his elephant away to the peanut vendor.

Angel and Roland approached as Mama bent to pick up the compressed piece of steel that was once a deadly weapon. "That," she told them with a glow in her eyes, "is what my God can do for those who trust and rely on Him. I think it's safe to say you won't be hearing from those two ruffians around here again."

And with a smile directed to both Roland and Angel, she left.

They stared after her, mouths agape. He was the first to recover.

"I guess she told us."

Angel dazedly nodded. Becoming conscious that she still held his arm, she dropped her hand from his sleeve, also realizing she didn't want to let go.

"Angel. . ." He seemed intent, even somewhat nervous as he fully turned to her. "Is there any chance that. . ."

She moistened her lower lip anxiously as he spoke. He paused, his eyes dropping to her mouth.

". . .I could kiss you?"

His words came quiet, a quick exhalation of breath, stunning her, appearing to stun him, and she wondered if that was what he intended to say.

She felt her head nod as though it wasn't a part of her.

His eyes flicked a little wider in surprise and with something else she couldn't read, something that made her heart pound. His fingertips touched her jaw and chin, lifting it higher. Her breath stopped, and then he lowered his lips to hers. They were warm, gentle, and though he kept the contact brief, she wished his kiss could have gone on forever.

He pulled away to look into her eyes, seeming to read her wish there. But before he could fulfill it and their lips could meet a second time, a man called out, "Make way! Make way!"

Startled apart, they barely missed being run over by a Gilly Wagon full of prizes. Nor did Angel miss the smirk that the carny pushing the wagon delivered to them, and she realized, her face burning, that they still stood in the middle of the midway, with people walking by on each side. A few had stopped to watch, as if they were one of the acts.

"Maybe we should save this conversation for another time," Roland suggested.

"I think that would be wise."

They exchanged nervous smiles, and he took her lightly by the elbow, escorting her to her ticket booth.

After the evenings occurrences, she couldn't steady her thoughts to make sense of them, the sensation in her head and heart like emotional bumber cars crashing in one another.

Friendship with Roland. That was all she wanted. All they could have. Wasn't it? She couldn't afford to get close! *Oh, but his kiss* . . . .No! It would be a mistake to get involved. A horrible mistake. Not only because of his family but because of hers. Like Romeo and Juliet, this could only end in tragedy because of their families: one, a warring family who murdered all who opposed them, and the other, a family with a mother who at one time in history anyone might have tried to murder. All because of fear . . .and being different. And then there was. . .the beast who sired Angel and made her into what she was.

If any two people were doomed from the start, it was she and Roland.

As she looked into his dark, mesmerizing eyes when he told her good night, she harshly reminded herself of those facts. But when he held her hand and kissed her fingers in farewell, her traitorous heart began to melt.

eleven

"You're a ninny, Angel. A complete and utter fool."

Angel chastised herself as she sewed the last seam of Posey's wedding gown. From Mama she had acquired pretty seed pearls and white sequins and was eager to surprise her little friend with a delicate pattern of posies she would scatter along the bodice.

"Planning your wedding?" Cassie grinned as she stepped into the car.

"Funny."

"It wasn't intended to be. News flash, Angel—you may be the only one who doesn't realize it, but Roland is mad about you. And if you look in the mirror at your face every time his name is mentioned, you'll see he's not the only one whose head and heart are in a whirl."

That's what troubled her.

"You're doing it now! Your eyes are bright, and your cheeks are flushed."

Ignoring her friend's gentle teasing, Angel thought over the past few weeks. She had allowed too many walks with Roland, too many occasions of letting him escort her to work, and too many conversations shared after the show closed, when they stood beneath the moon in the living lot and spoke of their workdays and other areas of their lives. Sometimes she foolishly accepted his kiss good night. He never pushed her, never deepened the moment into something stronger, though she sensed he wanted to. But it failed to matter. Her emotions had spiraled into something she didn't recognize, her heart becoming entwined with his. And when he kissed her and held her, she felt as if she'd ceased to be a part of the carnival world and somehow shared a place all alone with him. She'd found a sense of purpose and peace during her time here with Roland. Having never known such feelings before, she didn't want them to end.

Frowning, she remembered Cassie's words about true love. No. Surely not that. She was inexperienced in such matters. But surely. . .not that.

Yes, Roland was different from other men, despite his family roots. Unobserved, she had watched during their first week in New Milford and seen him dig deep into his pocket for coins to hand out to Sam, the poor boy they'd met in town, and his two friends, so that they could all enjoy the carnival. She'd watched him quietly lend aid to whoever needed it without being asked, and though at first he clearly didn't fit in, he began to adapt to his surroundings—and appeared to enjoy the change—and gain others' trust. He didn't seem to mind getting his hands dirty or even miss the expensive silk suit he wore when she first met him.

But he was only a friend!

Who are you kidding? her heart taunted. *Friends don't kiss good night.*

You're a fool, Angel, her mind scolded. *You know why you shouldn't get involved. Are you insane?*

"Are you all right?"

"What?" Angel startled then realized what Cassie asked. "Fine. How are things between you and Chester?"

"Much better since the night I did my trick." Cassie regarded her oddly but didn't push. She seemed more animated than usual, fluttering around the railcar like a golden butterfly, and had yet to take a seat. "Papa now sees Chester can be serious and isn't just a funny man—they actually agreed on something, to disagree with me about doing my stunt. Can you believe it?" She laughed.

"Cleaning the horses' stalls for a month as punishment in going against Papa's orders, I didn't mind so much," Cassie pondered aloud. "Nor did I really mind him insisting I wait to do the stunt again until I perfect my timing—he's right. I need more practice, though I knew I could do it that night, despite what everyone said. And really, I'm glad I did. It made me feel stronger, like the woman I am. Not like the little girl I was, who couldn't make her own decisions and always needed Papa to tell her what to do. I think he's finally beginning to see that I've grown up. But that night did more than I believed possible. Since Papa agreed to let me see Chester, he got brave enough to ask Papa for his blessing. And Papa agreed." She glowed as she held out her left hand where a modest ring circled her finger. "See?"

"Cassie!" Angel squealed, setting aside Posey's gown to hug her friend, who sank down beside her. "Why didn't you tell me any of this before?"

"You don't know how much I wanted to! But Chester and I agreed to keep things secret, at least until we were sure how it would all turn out. We're getting married the week after Posey's wedding. I didn't want to steal from her day."

"So soon?"

"We've known each other forever, it seems, and have both wanted this for twice that long." Cassie giggled. "We'll be staying on, so Mahoney won't lose us as part of his meal ticket. And you and I will still be close." She grabbed Angel's hands. "Just think, I'm going to be Mrs. Chester Summerfield in two weeks' time!"

Angel felt thrilled for Cassie, but dismal in her own loss. Her two closest friends, Posey and Cassie, had found their true loves, and that made the bite of Angel's loneliness harder to swallow. . .though her heart again whispered it didn't have to be that way.

"It's getting late." She stood quickly. "I need to take this dress to Posey so she can try it on and I can make any alterations."

"You sure spend a lot of time over there." Cassie looked at her thoughtfully.

Angel shrugged. "They've become my friends. Though Gunter still gives me the willies."

Cassie laughed. "Gunter gives everyone the willies; it's just his nature."

"But I feel so sorry for him, how that gypsy carnival did all that to him when he was younger, inflicting all those tattoos and piercings against his will then caging him like an animal." She shuddered.

"That he even opened up to you was a giant step for the man. Harvey, too. He's always been a tough nut to crack, bitter and angry all the time, but even he seems different since you came."

"Well, he did get fresh with me my first week here. . . ." Angel remembered his dumbfounded look when she snubbed him. "I told him if he'd behave, I'd consider being a friend, but that if he didn't rein in his octopus arms, I'd smack him over the head with the stool I was carrying so fast he wouldn't know what hit him. He hasn't given me a problem since."

"You said that to him?" Cassie laughed. "I would have loved to hear that." Her eyes twinkled. "But really, Angel, being serious—you have a sweetness and sincerity mixed with a strength I never noticed when we became bunk mates. To be honest, I wasn't sure about you. I thought you were shy and maybe a little conceited, thinking you were better than any of us."

"Oh my!" Angel laughed. "That couldn't be further from the truth. I was nervous though."

"Maybe so. But I was wrong to judge you so quickly and harshly. You're none of what I thought."

"I am so glad I left my aunt's to come here. Meeting all of you has made such a difference in my life."

Cassie grew pensive. "Do you still think about finding your mother?"

At the leap to such a question, Angel regarded her oddly. "Why would you ask such a thing?"

"I just hoped that maybe, now that you've found a home with us, you were finally happy."

"I am, but—"

"Knock, knock." Chester's jovial voice came from outside the railcar.

Cassie lit up like she'd swallowed the sun and hurried to open the door. "Chester."

"Hey, honey bun. Thought I'd take my wifey-to-be out to lunch at a genuine restaurant."

"Only if you promise never to call me 'wifey' again." Her mock-stern features melted into a smile, and she allowed him to swing her down from the car, his hands at her waist. They shared a quick kiss, seeming to forget all about Angel.

She looked on, amazed to note the evident changes in their relationship, which they clearly no longer hid, and she grinned. "I hear congratulations are in order."

With Cassie's arms still wound around his neck, Chester glanced Angel's way, his face reddening. "You got that right." He looked into Cassie's eyes. "And I finally got my Cassie."

She sighed dreamily. "Now *that* you can call me till the end of time."

"We best hurry so we can get back, honey. Bye, Angel!"

They both waved to her and hurried away, hand in hand.

"Bye," she whispered, and for some foolish reason, she struggled with the insane urge to cry.

❧

Three nights later Roland stopped in front of Angel's ticket booth, with Chester beside him.

"Oh. . .hello?" Curiously she glanced from one to the other. Worry suddenly clouded her eyes. "Nothing bad about Cassie?"

"No," Chester assured her. "She's fine. Mama thought you'd like to see more of the carnival while it's in progress, and I'm here to take you and Roland on a tour."

"What about your own show?"

"I can close this one night. You two have been with us almost a month now, and it's time you saw the carnival as spectators, not workers. Jezzie's going to man your booth again."

"Hi, Angel!" As if on cue, the girl appeared, out of breath. She always seemed to be running to or from somewhere.

"Hi, Jezzie." Angel handed her the key to the strongbox from the pocket of her skirt. "Thanks for doing this."

"Oh, I don't mind. I love working the Hollars' booth. When there's a lull, I like to slip in and watch the show. I wish I could do what Cassie does. She's so good." It was evident Cassie had a doting fan.

Angel smiled at the girl and turned to Roland and Chester. "I'm ready."

"Then we're off!"

Roland held out his hand to her.

Angel looked at his open palm, indecision on her face. In that awkward moment Roland wasn't sure if he should drop his hand to his side or keep it held aloft and frozen like some ridiculous tailor's dummy. The seconds seemed endless. Just as he was about to pull away with some pithy wisecrack to cover his embarrassment, she slid her hand quietly into his.

There was absolutely no reason his heart should feel as if it had just risen to his throat and pounded there. At the touch of her soft, warm skin against his own, he felt as if he'd been given a prize far better than anything the carnival could offer.

Chester stood beside Roland, an annoyingly smug grin

dancing on his face as they began strolling down the midway.

"Should I ask Cassie to make it a double wedding?" he whispered so Angel couldn't hear.

"Keep quiet, man." Roland darted a look at her face, just in case, relieved to see her interest wrapped up in one of the game booths.

The irritating grin did not leave his so-called friend's face as he began pointing out areas of interest. His previous words, however, lodged deep inside Roland's heart, and he found himself turning them over a number of times as they walked. *Marriage*? To *Angel*? Would she ever consider such a prospect? Did he want that?

Regardless of Chester's warning that many games were rigged to deflect the amount of winners, Angel exhibited a desire to visit the dart-throwing booth. "I blew up so many of those balloons I'd like the chance to try to deflate some," she explained with a grin.

"It's your nickel." Chester shrugged. "But I warn you, he uses darts with dull tips."

The agent behind the counter smiled widely to see Angel and greeted her with sincere preference. She didn't pop more than one balloon but clearly enjoyed herself in the attempt.

"For you," the agent said, handing her a small plush lion, one of the top prizes.

"But. . ." She looked at the toy in confusion. "I didn't win."

"If not for your help, I would have had to blow up all them confounded balloons myself. I may be full of hot air"—he winked—"but I don't have the lung power for that no more."

"Thanks, Fletcher." She awarded him with a sweet smile that made the agent beam.

If the man weren't at least two decades older than Angel, Roland might have been a little resentful of his focused attention. Who was he kidding? He was. And he had no right to be, which, for some reason, irritated him further.

"The carnival is certainly different from what I expected," Angel said as they walked away. "My aunt led me to believe it was quite horrifying."

"The perverse acts you might have associated with carnivals are in the bygone days of its glory," Chester replied like a true tour guide. "Ever since it's become more of a family event, things are kept pretty clean. Though you still have your shysters to avoid." He nodded back to the game booths.

They ate hot dogs and pretzels and popcorn until no one had room for more.

"Want to try the rides?" Chester motioned to the lot where the Ferris wheel stood. Angel's attention fixed on a covered musical dais with gilded horses.

"I love the carousel," she said wistfully then laughed, placing a hand to her flat stomach. "But right now I don't think I could stand anything in motion."

They continued down the midway and ran into Blackie and Ruth selling balloons. Blackie gave Angel a blue one, refusing to take her penny, and the clownish duo went into one of their performances, drawing a crowd. Angel laughed so hard Roland noted tears coming out of her eyes. Afterward Blackie passed around a hat that several threw coins into, and Roland did as well. It had been worth the dime, and more, to see Angel happy.

A trip to the crazy house of mirrors and a sack of peanuts shared rounded out their fun, when suddenly Angel stopped, as though frozen.

"Angel?"

She stared, and Roland followed her line of vision. His heart clenched as he recalled the day they had stood before this tent and she'd behaved in the same manner. THE HUMAN FREAK SHOW, the banner above proclaimed.

The whole spectacle disgusted him. The way these people

were treated reminded him of his grandfather's cold manipulation over others and their inability to break free, acting as marionettes to his callous whims. Roland knew Angel had befriended the people there, and he put a hand to her elbow.

"Come on, Angel. We don't have to see this."

"No." A determined expression crossed her face. "I need to."

twelve

Angel knew her reply surprised Roland, but she had to see, had to know. She couldn't understand her desire, but neither could she quench it.

"Step right up, and see the most amazing creatures to walk the face of the planet. That's right, folks, we're going to bring them out here, all for free, just to let you get a peek. Watch the entranceway for the amazing Siamese Twins, the Leprechaun Couple, the Illustrated Man, and that's not all . . . ." The barker paced the stage, his energy and ballyhoo swiftly bringing in a crowd.

"That's Tucker." Chester's voice became grim. "A seedy fellow. I've had dealings with that man. Trust me when I say to steer clear of him."

Angel had also had dealings with Tucker, none of them pleasant. When she brought Posey and the others their meals, he had tried to rush her off. The first time, she submitted. But his maltreatment of her friends ignited a righteous anger that burned deep, and the next time, she refused to leave, ignoring the ill-mannered beast to stay and talk with the other women and help, usually by stitching up tears or sewing on buttons for any of the performers who needed it. Tucker soon realized she wasn't the hindrance he thought and allowed her to stay. Angel would have done so without his gruff permission.

"Why do they let him do that to them?" she asked sadly as he spun his thoroughly demeaning ballyhoo for Rita and Rosa, making them sound more like monsters than people, and the two women stepped out of the tent on cue. "*Why?* It's just not right!"

Chester shook his head; he had no answer. Roland's eyes filled with sympathetic concern as he regarded Angel. His hand still at her elbow, his thumb caressed her arm through her sleeve. His gesture warmed her, and she sensed he understood her heartache. Yet even he couldn't begin to comprehend the extent of it.

Was this how her mother had been treated? Forced to stand on a platform as a "peculiar specimen of nature" and made to endure belittling remarks from a crass talker, who poked and prodded, while an insensitive crowd gawked as if she were something less than human? How could she have borne such humiliation, night after night?

Angel's eyes brimmed with hot tears.

She'd known the sting of scorn and embarrassment from her aunt and cousins, but this was much worse. Perhaps at times her rebellious tendencies invited their nasty behavior. But these people, these friends, had done nothing to warrant such ridicule! Rita and Rosa had been born into a life of poverty. Their parents, had they wanted the twins, couldn't have afforded an operation to separate them. Why were life and people so cruel? How could Mama allow such a thing to go on at her carnival? How could her own mama have had any spirit left to go on living, especially after her attacker defiled her in the most vicious of ways. . . .

"Angel?"

A tear followed by another rolled down her cheek. She heard Roland's sharp intake of breath and felt him gather her close, his strong arm around her shoulders, protective and warm. Grateful as she was for his consideration, she felt numb and frozen.

How easily she might have been one of them, up on that platform, raped of all self-worth in the cruel and careless spiel of a barker's belittling words. And yet, she *was* one of them. Her face and form may have escaped physical imperfection, but in her soul she'd struggled with the contempt of others her entire life. By the bond of blood in being her mother's child, she identified with Rosa and Rita and others like them more than she did with those who stood on the opposite side and rudely gaped. She felt so utterly alone.

"That's called building the tip—the crowd," Chester said solemnly. "Next, he'll turn the tip, with a ballyhoo to send them running to buy tickets to see more."

"Let's get out of here." Roland moved to draw her away, his arm still around her, but she resisted his gentle pull.

She needed to remain through all of this until the crowd went inside for more, needed to experience what her mother had lived. In that way she hoped to begin to understand the heart of the woman who'd given away her child.

"I'm staying." She glanced up. In Roland's eyes she spotted the strength and support she so desperately craved. Not once in his expression had she seen any sign of curious revulsion, apparent on every other face looking toward that awful tent platform.

"Please stay with me?" Her soft request was unnecessary; she knew he wouldn't leave her. But she needed to hear his answer.

"I'm not going anywhere." His firm response warmed her cold insides, while making her shiver with uncertainty, for it implied so much more than the here and now, something she wasn't sure she could ever handle. "I'm here for you, Angel."

She nodded in gratitude, casting aside all doubt and logic, and her heart clung to his promise.

※

In one night everything changed.

Roland wasn't sure what to make of the changes in Angel, but he hoped they would last. Aside from the few kisses he'd been unable to refrain from, he'd made no overtures to a close relationship. And though her nervousness when near him didn't vanish completely, she was nowhere near as jumpy as she'd been their first week together.

But that wasn't what amazed him.

Over the weeks that followed their little carnival participation with Chester, Roland had watched Angel begin to blossom, seeming to find peace within. The carnies all loved her, women and men both, to his chagrin. With selfish gratitude he watched her gently turn down interest after romantic interest, and his heart surged with hope when she didn't refuse his own tender advances of affection. Inwardly that affection grew in strength each day.

Though the two recent weddings sparked a desire he'd never had, the sparkle left her eyes and sadness settled there after first Posey then Cassie tied the knot with their fellows. He assumed Angel missed her bunk mate and felt lonely for companionship. Roland was only too happy to act as a stand-in.

He had never seriously considered marriage until Chester's wisecrack. Since then it seemed to be all he thought about. Regardless of the fact that he was hiding from his mobster family and trying to carve a new life, one in which he'd found, to his surprise, satisfaction and the same peace Angel had, he'd never planned to live out the rest of his days in bachelorhood. When the time was right and he felt assured he could keep her safe, he wanted a wife. And he was fairly certain he knew her identity.

During a night in Kent, once the fairgrounds closed to visitors and the nightly chores were done, Roland approached Angel at the ticket booth.

"Take a walk with me?"

Angel's face brightened. She closed up the strongbox, locking it. "I just need to drop this off at Pearson's car first."

They took the night's earnings to the disgruntled man, who never once looked up from his account book and barely paid them a moment's notice, mumbling something that could have been *good night* or *get lost* to their parting words.

Roland shrugged as they walked away, and she giggled. He took her hand in his as he'd done often lately, since the night of "the change." She offered no resistance.

"You look like you had a good day." He appreciated how the silver moonlight brought out a cool sheen to her hair when they weren't walking near the incandescent yellow bulbs of carnival lights, which conversely brought out touches of silky red warmth.

"I did. Cassie went with me at lunchtime when I delivered meals to Posey and the others. We all had a lovely talk." She grew pensive as she focused on something in the distance. "I finally had the chance to talk to Mama again, in private. I asked her why she had such a degrading show at her carnival. Even if all the other carnivals have them, it still didn't seem like she would, as caring and sensitive as she is."

When it didn't appear as if she would continue, Roland prodded, "What did she say?"

"She doesn't like it either. But she said at least here she can visit them, treat them with kindness and respect, help them out—something they might not get with another carnival. Tucker doesn't care about them, to see to their needs." Angel frowned at that. "She did tell me it was their choice to be in the show; apparently she asked each of them in private when they first joined the carnival, telling Tucker she would never condone any form of slavery if he held them against their will. Sadly they were all here because of choice, feeling that's all life has to offer them. Mama says she hopes by giving her friendship and prayers she can help make a difference. She has a very soft spot in her heart for those who work in that tent. One of the previous performers was a woman who led her down the path to find God, and she owes everything to that woman."

Roland nodded, recalling when Mama had told him the same thing.

"How do you feel about them? You never did say."

Her question came quiet, but Roland got the distinct impression a lot hinged on his response. "I never really gave it much thought. You're asking, what? Do I think them freaks of nature? Am I disgusted by their appearance?"

She tentatively nodded.

"The answer is no. Especially not after getting to know Jim, probably one of the smartest men I've ever met. His knowledge of the classic literary works is incredible. Did you know he's memorized every work of Shakespeare? Still, I can't help but feel curious about how they got that way and pity them for how they're treated."

His sincerity brought a faint smile from her. "Jim and I were discussing *Romeo and Juliet* several weeks ago. He recited parts of it for me."

At her odd words and the even odder note in her voice, he looked at her. "Oh?"

"It's a very sad story." She sighed. "Two people in love but with everything going against them."

They approached the carousel. The horses no longer revolved, the customers gone for the day, but bright lights from within the dais bounced off its huge, mirrored column. Lively calliope music played from a door within.

She looked at the gilded horses, her face alight with wonder. "I've always loved the merry-go-round. . . ." She stopped suddenly, focused.

"Angel?" His fingers went to her chin, bringing her eyes to meet his.

"It's nothing. A memory that's gone before it even begins." She gave a nervous laugh and shrugged. "So what's your favorite thing about the carnival?"

Wishing to erase every hurtful memory she'd ever suffered, he looked into her beautiful wide eyes that shone like blue midnight in the dark evening. The feelings he'd cautiously pushed aside for weeks rose to fill his heart.

"You."

At his whisper, her lips parted in surprise, and he leaned in to her, his mouth taking in their soft warmth. He cupped her face, slowly brushing his lips over hers more than once, unable to resist her sweetness. Her arms wrapped around his neck, and she breathed a sigh of delight, which enticed him to press closer and deepen the kiss, giving in to his desire to love her. . . .

Her legs soon gave way. He lowered his arms around her back, pulling her firmly against his body to steady her. It took every bit of willpower for him to finally break free from her delicious mouth and let her go.

She wobbled a step. His hands reached out to support her. She blinked up at him, unfocused, her breathing as rapid as his. He had not meant to take their kiss so far, and he winced at the trace of anxiety he saw beneath the longing in her eyes.

"Angel, you must know you mean the world to me." He brushed her hair from her temple. "I want this—us—to have a relationship like Chester and Cassie have. Like Posey and Darrin—"

"M–m–marriage?"

He saw the thought terrified her and dropped his hands away from her, working to get his emotions under control. What was wrong with him? He was rushing this, ruining everything.

"One day maybe. If you want it." He swallowed hard, fighting the impulse to kiss her again, gently this time, to hold her close to his heart and eliminate whatever doubts were running through her lovely head. "I want us to be more than friends," he finished lamely.

Her eyes, if wide before, grew enormous. She backed up a step.

"Th–this is so s–sudden. I. . .have to go. I need time to. . . to think."

"Angel. . ."

"No, don't." She shook her head, backing up another step. "Please, Roland. Not right now. I. . ." With a pained expression, she whirled around and hurried away.

❧

Not right now. Not *ever*!

She moved without really seeing, anxious to reach her railcar.

"Angel?"

Blinking hot moisture from her eyes, she noticed Cassie and Chester strolling arm in arm. She couldn't form a greeting, afraid it would come out as a sob.

"Angel, what's wrong?"

She shook her head and walked faster. Within moments she felt Cassie's arm around her waist—glad for the support, wishing to be alone, wondering why Roland didn't follow, relieved and disappointed he hadn't.

Heaven help her, she was a mess.

He had never, *never* kissed her like that! And while her heart had raced with the desire for more, was still racing, her mind callously scolded her for letting it come to this.

Once he found out the truth, once he knew. . .

He could never know.

"There now," Cassie said as she stepped up with Angel into the railcar, "tell me what happened. Did you have a fight with Roland?"

Angel laughed without humor. So far from a vocal fight yet a powerful confrontation that destroyed all hope. She looked at her dear friend, wishing she could tell her everything but feeling unable to. She cried harder.

Cassie pulled her close, holding and rocking her as if she were a child. Angel brushed her tears away with resolve. She never cried. But then, little in her life had mattered so much.

"I have to leave the carnival."

"What?" Cassie's eyes rounded in distress. "Why?"

"I can't explain. I just. . . I have to go." She gulped down another sob. "I'll go back to searching for my mother. It was one of the reasons I left my aunt's in the first place."

A calm but determined expression crossed Cassie's face.

"Angel, about that. . ."

"I've earned enough so I won't have to do what I did before. Did I tell you?" She forced a laugh. "I stowed aboard a train. That's how R—Roland and I met." She couldn't even say his name without stumbling over it.

"Angel. . ."

"It's for the best. I know it is." It had to be.

"Angel, I know where your mother is."

thirteen

Angel stared, unseeing. Her mind went numb with shock.

Cassie's skin flooded with shamed color. "I didn't tell you at first, because. . .well, honestly, I didn't know if I could trust you. Lila's been hurt by so many. And I thought you were one of them who hurt her before."

Angel remembered to breathe. "She *worked* here?"

Cassie nodded. "I didn't know her well, but she was so sweet, and I. . ." Her gaze shifted to her lap. "I'm sorry. When it seemed you'd found happiness with us, I thought it best just to leave things be. But I know you now. You really care. You don't like seeing them hurt. I was only trying to protect her from that possibility."

Angel's initial anger at her friend's deception faded in the glow of hope that she knew her mother. "Where is she?"

"I don't know. I'm sorry, I really don't."

"But I thought you said—"

"I don't, but Mama does."

For the third time that night, Angel felt as if she'd been struck.

Mama knew? All this time?

"Please don't be angry. Please forgive me. . . ."

Angel nodded absentmindedly, her thoughts rushing ahead. "We'll talk. Later. I have to find Mama now."

Her battered emotions in a precarious tailspin, Angel left Cassie and ran to the front of the train and Mama's car.

The woman often helped others, and Angel worried she might not be there. She had waited what seemed her entire lifetime for this moment, but a matter of minutes she

143

didn't think she could bear. Thankfully a light shone from the crack, and Angel pounded on the door.

"Angel?" Mama said in surprise as she opened it.

Out of breath, Angel strived for control. "I want to know where my mother is. And I know you can help me."

Mama remained composed. "I've been expecting you."

That was the last thing Angel thought to hear.

"Come in, child." Mama opened the door wider, and Angel woodenly stepped inside. "I assume you spoke to Cassie? I spoke with her earlier about telling you. That it was time. And I imagine you're feeling very betrayed right now. But I want you to consider this: Your mother lived with that emotion daily, and I couldn't allow her to be hurt again. You see"—and here Mama smiled gently, smoothing her hand against Angel's hair like she was a little girl—"your mother was the one who led me to the Lord."

Angel sank to a nearby chair, her legs suddenly useless. "My mother did?" Her voice came whispersoft.

"Yes. And especially after hearing her story, I owed it to Lila to protect her interests."

Her story? "Tell me. Please. I know so little about her. Only what my aunt told me." Which was all suspect.

Mama seemed to consider then shook her head. "It's not my place. It's your mother's."

"Then you'll tell me where she is?" Angel pleaded.

"Now that I've received her permission to, yes."

Stunned, Angel inhaled a shaky breath. "Sh–sh–she knows I'm l–looking for her?"

"I called her from town. Told her about you. Asked what she wanted to be done."

"And?"

Mama picked up a piece of paper from a table. "This is where you can find her."

Angel took the slip as if it were the most fragile, expensive china. Here. . .now. . .the answer she'd been praying for! Dread and anticipation fought for control in her heart.

"I guess it's safe to assume you'll be leaving us?" Mama asked as Angel continued staring at the address. At Angel's nod, Mama sighed. "I can't say I won't be sorry to see you go, but I know it's the right thing. It's high time the past was fixed."

Angel didn't ask what she meant, only stared at the worn face and merry eyes of the slight woman who'd been an inspiration.

"Thank you, Mama. For. . .everything. And. . .I. . .I do understand." For the most part, she did. Mama and Cassie had only been trying to protect Lila, just as she had wished to shield Posey, Rita, and Rosa from others' cruelty. That they thought Angel could bear such malice toward her own mother stung a little, but then Angel herself hadn't known how she would feel around those considered different.

Now, in knowing, she no longer feared how she would react to her mother's appearance. It was how she would respond to her explanations that chilled her.

Mama Philena held out her arms in understanding, and Angel numbly walked into them, hugging her close.

ֶ

Unable to sleep, Roland stood at the door of his boxcar, a cool breeze hitting his face. Angel wasn't the only one to lose a bunkmate, and though Roland missed his wisecracking friend, he felt grateful for these quiet moments to think.

He had never wanted for anything, though he hated the ruthless methods his family used to obtain wealth. Yet Angel, deprived of most worldly possessions, had shown Roland that for all his affluence, he'd had nothing. Here, at this rinky-dink carnival, he had discovered a measure of happiness, found out who he was, and learned what truly mattered. Who would have believed it? Angel was everything to him, and he didn't want to live without her. No matter how slow he must take things, he would. He had no intention of scaring her away ever again.

A sudden rectangle of yellow light glowing on the ground brought his attention to the left. His eyes widened in disbelief.

Angel had descended from her boxcar, set down her suitcases, and turned to give Cassie a long hug.

"What the. . ." He blinked. She was leaving?

His initial shock gave way to anger. Again, in the dead of night, she was sneaking away into the countryside she knew nothing about and putting herself at risk. Was ever such a reckless woman created?

With a growl of frustration, he tied on his shoes, slipped his silk jacket over his carny work clothes, and pulled on his hat. His manner of dress was bizarre, but there was no time to change. Besides the clothes on his back, he took nothing but the wages he'd earned. Compared to his former weekly allowance, it was a pittance, yet it was also a king's ransom, due to the burden lifted off his soul for not spending blood money.

He followed her at a distance, watching her move toward the boxcar where Posey and her husband slept. She knocked and spoke to the tiny blond who opened the door. Suddenly she, too, was wrapped in Angel's hug, which Posey returned just as fiercely. The same ritual happened at Rita and Rosa's car, leaving Roland no doubt as to Angel's intent.

"You going after her?"

Mama's quiet voice coming from near the tree he stood behind startled him. "I can't let her go off by herself."

"I wouldn't expect so. Your feelings are plain to see. Always have been." She patted his arm. "A word of advice. She's had a bad shock so might be touchy. Handle her with care. . .and with caution."

He wondered if Angel's shock was due to his earlier lapse

of self-control; he also wondered if Angel had told Mama about it and felt a twinge of guilt. "I don't like leaving you in the lurch like this. Mahoney isn't going to like it either."

"Don't you worry about my son. I own the carnival, remember?" She winked and patted his cheek. "You just go and do what needs doing. Take care of her, Roland. She's a dear, but I don't need to tell you that."

He nodded, and they watched Angel move away. After a farewell hug and thanks to Mama, Roland followed.

He trailed his misguided Angel to the train depot before she suddenly whirled around, her angry eyes pinning him to the spot.

ಜ

Angel had sensed him earlier but had written the feeling off as nerves. Yet there he stood, not twenty feet away, dark, handsome, and oh so dangerous. . . .

Not to her life but to her heart.

He approached her. "Nice night for a walk."

His tendency to initiate conversation with the understated would have made her laugh if she hadn't felt so hollow.

"What are you doing here? Please tell me that you're not following me again."

"I could ask you the same." His eyes glimmered with frustration and hurt. "You don't have to run away, Angel. It was only a kiss. I promise I'll behave if you'll just come back."

She didn't know whether to laugh or cry. His explanation of *only a kiss* and his vow to behave brought an irrational pang to her heart. He thought his kiss sent her packing? Though it had shaken her to her core, making her feel things no decent girl should, she would never admit that to him. Perhaps her aunt was right, and she wasn't decent at all.

"It's not about. . .the kiss." Even saying the words made her breathless, and she condemned her awkward tongue. "I'm not that childish. It's just. . .something came up. And

I would appreciate it if you'd just. . .go back to the carnival. You're safer there than out here in the open—especially on a train, since your family owns an interest in the railroad!"

Concern touched his rich brown eyes. "Angel, what's wrong?"

She forced a calm she didn't feel, knowing he would never go if he suspected her pain. This man had been her friend, though she felt much more for him. But that wasn't his fault either, and he didn't deserve her antagonism.

She softened her tone. "I'm sorry I gave you a hard time, Roland. I—I hope you find a happy life and the peace you deserve. I'm fine. Really." She smiled, hoping to convince him. "The, um, family I told you about months ago? I've decided to visit. So you needn't worry any longer. I'll be fine." Before she could curb her instinct, she stepped forward and raised herself on her toes to press a kiss to his cheek.

Startled at what she'd done, she backed away, seeing the shock reflected in his eyes.

"G—good-bye."

Her heart pounding like a drum, she whirled away, almost running for the ticket window.

Brilliant, Angel, she chastised herself as she paid for the fare. *Well done. If anything, you just aroused his suspicion.*

She chanced a fleeting glance over her shoulder. Relief and despair vied for top billing when she saw he was gone.

It's what you wanted, she tried to convince herself as she thanked the ticket seller and moved down the platform to a bench to wait. Despite the heavy beating her emotions had taken, once she sat immobile, she grew sleepy. She jerked awake several times but couldn't keep her eyes open.

"Miss!"

She jolted awake to see a man shaking her shoulder.

"I think this is your train."

"Oh." She straightened and put a hand to her hat, her ticket still clutched in her other hand with the location visible. That must be how he'd known. "Thank you."

He smiled, tipped his hat, and walked away.

Once aboard, Angel grew restless. She found a seat beside a genial, older gentleman who talked about his grandchildren for quite some time. She displayed the right amount of interest, but his words made her sad. She would never have grandchildren, never have children. She couldn't. No decent man would have her.

That led her to think of Roland. Months ago, upon first meeting him, she would have labeled him as far from decent. But the truth was, he was nothing like his family, everything a girl could want, and all that Angel wished a man to be.

Dear God. . . . She had taken to praying in her head often since meeting Mama. *Can You please help me forget him? And to forget that I l–love him. . . .*

Her eyes opened wide in horror at the truthful plea of her heart.

Love him!

She sucked in a deep breath, feeling the sudden need for oxygen.

Yes. Love him, her heart confirmed. *What did you think these feelings were that you've been having?*

No, no, no! She couldn't love him! Because of what she was, because of who he'd been. A gangster's son. A Piccoli. But. . .but he had changed. She had seen him change.

Yet that didn't erase the cold, hard fact that she never could.

"Are you all right, my dear?" the kind gentleman asked in fatherly concern. "You look a mite peaked."

She offered an unsteady smile. "Y–yes. I. . .I haven't eaten. I think I'll check what the dining car has to offer."

"Of course." He stood for her to get by.

This time, at least, she didn't have to worry about luggage, since she was a paying customer and a porter had taken care of her things before she boarded. Asking for directions from a steward, she felt grateful she had every right to be there and again determined to refund the fare Roland had paid on her behalf.

Roland, Roland. . .again, Roland.

I have to stop thinking about him!

Yet as Angel entered the dining car and stood frozen in the doorway, she realized with breathless shock her wish would not be granted.

Roland Piccoli sat inside a booth, his gaze lifting from the newspaper he held and melding with hers.

fourteen

Roland watched Angel stand in the doorway as if she might turn and run. A wealth of expressions swept across her face—shock, disbelief, anger, uncertainty, acceptance, fear. But one he hadn't expected to see—relief and even, dare he think it, happiness—made him take in a stunned breath. He clung to those last two expressions as she stiffly approached.

"I told you not to follow me," she accused in a hoarse whisper.

He motioned across the table. "Won't you take a seat?"

She ignored him. "But here you are."

"Here I am."

"Why?"

He folded his newspaper. "Because I care."

"I told you I can take care of myself!"

"Yes, and through the past months I've seen that, more and more."

She blinked. "Then why did you follow me?"

"I told you when we were last together at the carnival." Her cheeks flushed as if she also thought of their kiss. "I care about you, Angel. *You.* I want to be with you. And I think you want the same thing."

Her gaze fell to the table. "I can't be your m—mistress." Her face flooded with color.

He stared, at a loss. "Did I ask you to be? Do you still have such a low opinion of me that you think I would? This isn't a movie, Angel." His tone was sober. "Despite what they show about gangsters, just because I come from a family of them doesn't mean I woo every pretty dame—lady," he corrected, remembering how she disliked the former word, "and take her to my bed." Her face flushed darker at his frank words. "Don't you get it?" He leaned across the table, his eyes never leaving hers as he reached for her hand. "I care, Angel, because I love you."

Her reaction wasn't what he expected.

Her face lost all the color that had rushed into it earlier, her eyes went huge, and she snatched her hand away.

"You can't love me," she choked out.

"Too bad. Because I do."

"No, you don't understand. . . ." She backed up a step. "You can't! Just—just leave me be, Roland. Please!"

She hurried out of the dining car.

He blinked, confused, then went after her. For the first time he noticed they'd drawn the interest of every patron there, but he didn't care. Something troubled her, and he wanted to know what it was.

Sneaking a peek at the destination on her ticket while she'd been dozing on the platform bench had been a cinch. Suggesting to a fellow passenger that the lady there might miss her train had produced the required results, as Roland watched from a safe distance and the man had roused her. But trying to get Angel to see the facts would take every ounce of reason and persuasion he possessed, along with help from above, if Mama was right and God did listen.

He never doubted God's existence. It just seemed hypocritical for his grandfather to attend mass in the morning and order some poor sucker's death in the afternoon, at times brought about by his father's own hand. With that kind of upbringing, Roland had quickly been jaded. But Mama Philena was a different story, living her belief, showing it in her actions. And even Angel, in her confused way, had been enlightening, admitting her own ignorance in matters of faith but sharing Nettie's verses and inspirational sayings, which seemed to help her.

He caught sight of Angel in the aisle of the second coach. She turned at his step, a plea in her eyes. "Please, Roland, don't do this."

"You can't keep running from life, Angel. At some point you have to stop." He gently took her elbow, guiding her past her seat and to an empty row a short distance away. He couldn't help but notice her tremble.

If he'd not been positive Angel shared his feelings, he might never have admitted his own. But he had seen the tenderness returned in her eyes more than once, had noticed her face light up when he would approach at the carnival. He had known since he first met her in his private car that she was hiding something, something she was afraid would now upset him, and he resolved to remain calm no matter what she revealed.

Not wanting her to feel closed in, he took the seat near the window, shifting his hold from her elbow to her hand, and pulling her into the row with him. She sank to the seat, her body stiff.

"Tell me what's got you so upset."

She shook her head, her eyes squeezing shut.

"Angel, darling. . .I want to help. Don't clam up on me."

"Why, Roland?" she bit out softly, her eyes still shut. "Why did you have to fall in love with me? Why'd I have to—I. . .I can't do this, don't you see? It's too hard."

"What's so hard about it? Love is a beautiful thing, so I've heard."

Her eyes flew open, and she glared at him. "You can't love me because of what I am."

"An angel in the flesh?" he gently teased in his confusion.

She didn't laugh. Pain flickered in her eyes, making him wish he could erase the last few seconds. "Angel, I'm sorry. I didn't mean to sound flip."

"It doesn't matter. Oh Roland, can't you please just walk away and pretend you never knew me?"

"Can you?"

His low, deep response brought tears swimming to her eyes.

"This wasn't supposed to happen," she sobbed softly.

He noticed the passengers staring across the aisle. He cursed public cars and wished for a private car, but to get one, he would have to reveal his identity, and he could never do that.

"Angel, whatever it is can't be that bad. It won't change my feelings for you—"

"Won't it?" She cut him off, a hysterical edge to her words. "You're so sure, but you don't know. My aunt said no decent man would have me, and she's right! You could never want me."

That she now classified him as decent cheered him, but her self-condemning words gave him pain. "Well, your aunt's wrong. Why would she say such cruel things to you?"

"You want to know why?" Her voice raised a notch. "Because she's right. She hates me. Hates what my mother is. What if I were to tell you that my mother was one of the freaks at the carnival—what then, Roland? Would you be so quick to tell me you still love me? You tolerated their presence, even accepted them, when so many couldn't, but could you really accept me and still love me if I told you that my mother was once a bearded lady at the carnival? Could you?"

She jumped to her feet. "Because she was," she whispered. "And she is. And that's who I'm going to see. My mother, who abandoned me as a baby because my aunt said she didn't want me anymore. And heaven only knows why I'm visiting her now, because I sure don't!"

Stunned speechless, he could only stare. A pained look of acceptance hardened her features, and she straightened, almost regal.

"I thought so. I imagine I won't be seeing you again, Roland. Have a nice life."

She turned and swept back in the direction of the dining car, ignoring the shocked passengers who watched her retreat, many of whom then sneaked glances back at Roland.

Still dumbfounded, he couldn't move as her condemning words played repeatedly in his mind. His eyes fell shut.

Oh Angel.

❧

Twisting her napkin in knots, Angel ignored her Danish and coffee. What seemed like hours had passed, and still she replayed their words.

She should never have told him those things. What would he have done if she'd told him everything? About being nameless. Illegitimate. Trash.

He probably would have run to the farthest coach from hers, she thought with a hoarse laugh that was more of a sob. She, who never once cried in what amounted to years, now always seemed to burst into waterworks like a fountain. If she'd had a better grip on her emotions, this wouldn't have happened. With a disgusted sigh she looked out the window, watching the miles rush past in the blur of the lush countryside.

At last the whistle sounded. The train slowed. A porter made his rounds, calling out the location.

Coventry. Her destination.

Her eagerness in her quest began to dissolve. She twisted the napkin tighter. This was a mistake. She shouldn't have come. What would she find? What would she learn? That her aunt was right? That no one cared about her and no one ever had?

Someone came to stand beside her. Expecting the waiter with the bill, she looked up. . . And she froze, all words lodging inside her throat.

Roland looked at her limp hands and took the mangled napkin from them, laying it on the table. "I believe this is where you and I get off."

"Roland?" she said dumbly, as if staring at a ghost.

He gave her a faint smile.

"But. . ." She tried to think. "You. . . Why?"

"What you said changes nothing." He took her hand, helping her from the table. "I just thought you needed some time alone."

She moved without thinking, without feeling, letting him guide her through the train. By the time he collected her luggage, she had recuperated enough to speak.

"You don't have to go with me."

"No, but I want to. If you'll let me."

She nodded, a powerful relief surging through her. She didn't want to confront her mother alone, feared the very thought, and craved his support.

They moved toward a waiting taxi. Suddenly she stopped. He looked at her, curious.

"I forgot to pay for my food!"

"I took care of it."

"Roland, thank you, but. . ." Her cheeks warmed. "I still haven't paid you back for the first time."

"As if I would let you," he growled with a smile that quickened her breath. "You don't owe me a thing, Angel. Not now. Not ever."

With that enigmatic reply, he helped her into the cab.

The drive tested every one of her frayed nerves. The countryside was beautiful with its pretty farms and trees in bloom, but with each mile she knew she was getting nearer to the encounter she had longed for and equally dreaded.

Feeling Roland's warm hand cover hers, she began to relax, then turned her hand in his and gripped it like a vise when the cab pulled into a dirt lane. A small red farmhouse with maples and pines beyond and a cornfield off to one side came into view.

They had arrived.

fifteen

Angel still had not let go of Roland's hand when the cab stopped in front of the farmhouse.

"It'll be all right," he said, trying to reassure her.

Will it? she thought when she caught sight of a slender woman in the doorway, a veil covering the lower part of her face. Angel didn't need anyone to tell her who this was: the same woman in the faded photograph of the album in her luggage. Lila.

Roland helped her from the cab. Angel stood motionless at the end of the walk and stared at the woman, who didn't move either. *I have her same curly, dark hair,* Angel thought distantly, followed by another thought, even more startling. *Why, she's beautiful.* Her eyes were huge and dark, her nose and brow above the veil, delicate and creamy white.

"You are Angel."

The vision spoke, and Angel gave a terse nod, noting how she didn't address her as Angelica. Had she first given her the nickname Angel preferred?

Lila held out a slim hand that trembled. Only then did Angel see how nervous the woman also was. "Please, won't you come inside?" Her voice was quiet and husky. "And your friend as well." She offered Roland the briefest of glances before looking at Angel again.

They followed her into a comfortable parlor. An elderly man with white whiskers sat in a chair. He looked up, an expectant but uncertain gleam in his eyes. Eyes the color of Angel's.

"This is my father. . .your grandfather."

"It's a pleasure, my dear." He took her hand in greeting.

Angel managed a reply, and the woman—her *mother*, though she still had a hard time thinking of her as such—excused herself to pour coffee. The man who was her grandfather talked amiably with Roland about the farm. When Lila returned, he invited Roland outside to see the land. Recognizing the polite maneuver to give them privacy, Angel smiled in reassurance at Roland, wordlessly assuring him that she would be fine when he cast a questioning glance her way.

"You must have many questions." Lila stirred her coffee once the men left.

Angel watched her, wondering if she would remove the opaque veil to drink, but she only lifted it slightly, making room for the cup.

"Why did you abandon me?" she asked tonelessly and without preamble. "I thought you were dead."

Lila's cup clinked to the saucer. "Th–that can't be true. Why would you think that?"

"You *didn't* abandon me?"

Lila winced. "Yes. I. . .I thought it best. Please, forgive me. I loved Bruce very much, and when he died of a brain hemorrhage, I was devastated. His sister—your aunt—despised me. We lived with her then, and she made it clear she didn't want me there any longer. She hated me for marrying her brother, and—and I knew the carnival would take me."

She gave a regretful sigh when Angel remained silent. "She convinced me it would be in your best interest to leave you with her. I think now she did it just knowing it would hurt me. And in remembering the difficulties and fear I had for you growing up at the carnival, I realized she was right. You did need a good home. Believe me, Angel, it was very hard to let you go." She began to reach for her hand but drew back. "I. . .I wanted to breach the gap between us, to try to right the wrong I'd done. You were twelve when I first wrote. But when I heard nothing,

I assumed you found a happier life without me in it. But why would you think I was dead? Because I stopped writing?"

Angel's blood went cold in shock then began to simmer with fury. "You wrote to me?" she whispered.

"Of course. Once a month. Up until three years ago, when your aunt wrote back, telling me. . .that you wanted nothing more to do with me. . .and to stop. . ." She gasped. "You never got the letters!" Her words came out hoarse in troubled realization.

"Aunt Genevieve told me you died when I was three." Angel's angry shock reverberated in her words. Her aunt had purposely kept them apart! Knowing that, and after what her mother now shared, Angel grew bold. "She was wrong. So were you. That's why I'm here."

Her mother's eyes swam with tears. She sat frozen in disbelief. "And now. . .now that you know. . .a–and see what I am? A sideshow freak?"

Angel's heart ached for her pain, and she answered with a question. "Do you wear that thing all the time?"

Her mother blinked in confusion. "The veil? No. I wanted to make you less uncomfortable. I—I have a deathly fear of razors, you understand, because of a bad accident with one as a child. I wear this when it's not just Father and me. He used to spurn me, too, but when I learned he was ill, I left the carnival to care for him, and God mended our relationship. Father doesn't mind me like this anymore." Her words rambled nervously.

Angel slipped out of the chair and knelt before her mother. Looking steadily into her eyes a moment, she reached up and gently pulled down the veil. Her mother tensed as Angel took in the short, curly beard then gasped as she curiously put her fingertips to it. It was soft and silky like everything about her. Angel's tears fell as her mother's did, and she lifted her eyes to the beautiful dark ones that regarded her with both dread and hope.

"I don't care what you look like either. Ever since I can remember, I've dreamed of you. Of you holding me and singing me to sleep. It was the only memory I had, and I thought it would be the only one I'd ever know."

Her mother tentatively cradled her face. "You would never close your eyes unless I sang to you. You were my Angel, my one bright light, and when I walked away that morning, the sunshine left, too."

"M–mama?" Angel whispered on a childlike sob, the years, the hurt, the anger all falling away.

Her mother swiftly embraced her, and memory sharpened to reality. Angel clutched her hard, crying in earnest, while her mother rocked her, holding her head to her breast. At the pure, sweet sound of the first lines to the lullaby from her dreams, Angel smiled through her tears, knowing no matter what the future held she would never be alone again.

※

Roland would never forget the stunned look of hopeful confusion on Angel's face when he told her he was staying, too, thanks to her grandfather's invitation. His own need to find work and hide somewhere secluded—and Birch Grove Farm, nestled in the middle of a small community, was about as secluded as you could get—coupled with his desire to help the aging minister aided his decision. Pastor Everett never had fully recovered his robust health after fighting pneumonia, so Roland was more than happy to help. Of course, being near Angel had been the main reason he stayed. So much of her previous behavior now made sense, and the only regret he had was that she hadn't trusted him sooner, though he couldn't blame her. He supposed if their situations had been switched, an ex-gangster wouldn't be his first choice as a confidant either.

Lila had dispensed with the veil, and Roland was amazed,

intrigued, and impressed that a woman who'd gone through so much suffering could have so stalwart a faith. To her soft-spoken question regarding the absence of her veil and his feelings on the matter, he casually assured her if they could tolerate his being a Piccoli, he could handle her beard, since his misfortune was the greater of the two. At his clear acceptance, any remaining tension dissolved, and Lila even laughed.

Everett expressed his faith with almost every sentence, opening up the Bible after suppertime and reading aloud then opening discussion. And Roland had a lot of questions.

"God is the Author of second chances," Everett told Roland one afternoon. "He gave one to me and my daughter, gave one to Lila and her daughter, and he's given you a second chance, too, son."

Roland couldn't argue with that. After his association with Mama, with his Angel, and now with her family, it wasn't long before one Sunday morning Roland made his decision.

He walked alone outside, his heart full with all he'd learned, and fell to his knees. The sun had just risen over the horizon, beaming hope. "I surrender all," he whispered, shaken. "All the pain and bitterness, all the anger. I choose to follow in Your footsteps, Lord. Please cleanse me of my many sins, wash me in Your blood. . .make me whole."

Caught up in a cushion of peace, what could have been minutes or hours later, he rose from the ground and felt as if a burden had literally dropped from his shoulders.

Mama was right. God did answer prayer.

ஐ

With each week that passed, Angel felt more at ease around her mother, whom she'd come to regard as a friend, and her grandfather, who became to her a wise teacher. His words inspired her to open her heart, to forgive her aunt and cousins, and not to judge herself harshly for things she couldn't help.

Her mother's story shocked and saddened her, and it was

with great care they delved into the question buried but always dominant in Angel's mind. Her father. Her mother admitted she never knew the identity of her attacker: The night had been dark, and she'd never seen his face. But she assured Angel that she was very much wanted and always had been.

"You were my lifeline, Angel. My reason to carry on. And such joy you gave me! Everyone at the carnival loved you . . . ." The more she spoke of Angel's early years, the more embers of memories faintly stirred: snippets of when her mother took her on her first ride on the carousel, after all pleasure seekers went home for the day and the operator gave in to the request of the man Angel had called Uncle Bruce before her mama married him.

Her grandfather was her counselor, her mother her inspiration, and Roland. . . She took in a deep breath as she envisioned the man who took up the greater portion of her thoughts. To her he meant the world. A friend, a protector, a confidant. Her reasoning finally gave in to her heart, admitting if only to herself that she was madly in love with him. She still hadn't told him her dark secret. With her mother's example, she came to accept what could never be changed. But would he feel the same about her once he knew? Of one thing Angel was now sure.

"Mama," she said late one Sunday afternoon, "I want what you and Grandfather have. What my friend Nettie and Mama Philena have." She smiled softly. "She said it was thanks to your influence that she found God. Will you show me how?"

Overjoyed, her mother prayed with her, and Angel added words of her own. "Thank You, dear Lord, for bringing me to this moment, for helping me find my mother, for Nettie, and for all those at the carnival who helped me understand what true beauty is. Please help my aunt and cousins to learn. And thank You for becoming the Father I never had."

Her mother squeezed her hands, her eyes teary, and Angel

hugged her, feeling as light inside as goose down.

"It's amazing," her mother said, "how the stubborn doings of one woman who came to visit the freak show that night long ago and wouldn't take no for an answer"—here she laughed—"could have initiated all this. God truly is a miracle worker, and just you wait and see, Angel, the plans He has for you!"

Thrilled and eager to share her news with Roland, Angel kissed her mother and hurried outdoors. She caught sight of his tall form, his back to her, his hands on his hips as he surveyed the land. Weeks of hard labor had strengthened his already lean, muscular frame, and her heart pounded in shy admiration at the sight of him.

Taking a shaky breath, she walked his way.

sixteen

"Roland?"

He turned, clearly lost in thought, but his eyes sharpened as they went to her face.

"Marry me, Angel," he whispered, his request as intense as his gaze.

"Wh–what?" She blinked, and all coherent thought vanished.

"Marry me." He gently grasped her shoulders. "You're all I think about, all I dream of. I want to share a life with you—this life. I want you to be my wife and the mother to my children." He looked at her lips that had parted in bewildered shock. "Angel. . ."

Her name came as a hoarse groan that warmed her lips as his mouth brushed hers. She yielded to him, pressing closer, having missed his touch so much. . . .

Then she remembered.

"No." At the flinch of pain in his eyes when she pushed him away, she quickly explained, "There's something I never told you." *Oh dear God, please. Please help me.* She didn't want to tell him, not like this. But she no longer had a choice. She loved this man. He had to know.

"I–it's about my parentage."

Roland relaxed. "Angel, Lila's condition doesn't bother me. I think she's a wonderful lady—"

His words brought some relief, but she shook her head to silence him. "It's about my father—my. . .lack of one."

She was going about this badly. There was no alternative but to blurt out the whole nasty truth and hope she wouldn't disgust him, hope he would at the very least remain her friend. Somehow she could learn to live with just that, as long as he didn't leave her life completely.

"So now you see," she said, as she finished her brusque retelling, "I'm nameless. Illegitimate. I can never change what I am, like you could change your circumstances. I don't have that choice."

To her absolute surprise, he moved forward and crushed her to him.

She'd thought she had no more tears left to cry.

He held her close, stroking her hair. "What you are is an angel."

At his gentle words, she pulled back to look at him. Sincerity shone in his eyes.

"You are what influenced me to change my life and escape the bonds of my family. Your grandfather told me that only God could bring something beautiful out of what was meant to be hurtful and wicked. And He did, Angel. He brought you." He smiled tenderly, and with his thumb he brushed away her fresh tears. "I consider myself fortunate to have been on the train the night you stumbled aboard. And I struggled over asking you to marry me for some time. I'm not exactly considered a great catch," he joked, bringing from her a soft smile. "The name Piccoli has struck fear into the hearts of many."

"You're nothing like your family!" she argued. "Any woman would be lucky to have you for a husband."

"Including you, Angel?" His fingertips brushed over her lips, causing her to tremble with new emotion. "Would you consider yourself lucky to be joined for life to someone like me? I think we're safe now. Your grandfather's faith has rubbed off on me; I trust that God will take care of us. But could you consider such a thing?"

"You're sure, after all I told you, that you still want me—"

Her words were cut off by his passionate kiss. A long time later he lifted his head, his dark eyes softened. "Does that answer your question?"

She nodded in breathless wonder, unable to speak.

"The truth is, my darling, I have never stopped wanting you."

They were married a week later, with her grandfather officiating and her mother acting as witness, along with a shy neighbor named Rose, whom Angel had met the previous week and welcomed to share in her joy. The private ceremony was all Angel desired, and she and Roland pledged unrehearsed vows, giving God the glory for the bizarre coincidences that had brought them together—events that perhaps were not coincidences at all—and for their blessed union, promising always to love, honor, and protect. Their vows were possibly unconventional, Angel thought, as she moved eagerly into her husband's arms for his kiss. . . .

But then, her dear family including herself, could hardly be considered typical.

Nor could her new husband who, in his delight to hear Angel pronounced his wife, firmly embraced her, lifting her off her feet and kissing her most soundly. Remembering the others, he abashedly broke the kiss and thanked them for their help, while letting Angel slide, breathless, back to the ground. Amid amused chuckles, the trio moved to the next room, to give them a moment's privacy. Eager to continue where they'd left off, Angel cradled Roland's head, lifting herself on her toes to press her mouth to his.

His arms fastened around her back, lifting her against his solid form, and she decided that *typical* was highly overrated. She wanted Roland Piccoli no other way.

epilogue

"Roland!"

Angel waved a letter and ran toward her husband as he walked home from the field. She threw herself into his arms, and he held her against him.

"What has you so excited, darling?"

"Cassie and Chester are coming! Oh, can you believe it? We'll get to see them again! The carnival train is coming east—to our town!" She pulled away and laughed, waving the letter. "If they can, I'd like them to come here to the farm and visit, but I do so want to go see them. To see everyone! Mama and Posey and Rita—and, oh, everyone!"

"Of course." He grinned at her exuberance.

"I cannot wait for the day to arrive!"

"I would never have guessed it."

"Oh you!" She slapped his shoulder then reached up to kiss him.

One afternoon later that week her mother received her own guest, sharpening Angel's curiosity when they immediately shut themselves up in her bedroom. She had yet to meet the woman from New York, and when Roland and her grandfather came in for supper, Mama and her guest were still behind the closed door. Angel knocked but found it locked. Her mother announced she wouldn't be coming to dinner, a strange note in her voice.

Concerned, Angel joined Roland and her grandfather for their meal of corn and bread with milk. Afterward her grandfather excused himself to do some reading.

"Roland, I'm worried." She cleared the dishes from the

table. "Mama's been acting odd lately."

"How so?"

"Anxious. . .distant."

He pulled her willingly into his lap, his arms linking around her waist. "You think it has something to do with her visitor?"

"That or the carnival. She hasn't seen them for years, and though only Mama, Cassie, and Chester will be coming, I'm sure it brings back bad memories."

His fingertips went beneath her chin. "What was it Nettie told you in her last letter? Not to borrow worry because there's more than enough to go around?"

"As if someone would actually want it?"

He chuckled and kissed her. Her heart so in love with this man, Angel pressed her hand to his cheek, eagerly deepening their kiss.

The sound of the door creaking open vaguely reached her ears.

"Angel? Roland? Could you come here a moment, please?"

Startled, Angel moved away, and Roland lifted her off his lap. She took his hand, and he squeezed it, helping to steady her nerves as they went to her mother's door.

❧

They looked in shock at the visitor, and then at Lila, whose jaw, delicate as the rest of her bone structure, was now clean-shaven. A faint white scar the length of a few inches lay visible on her jaw line; despite the flaw, she was easily one of the most beautiful women Roland had ever seen. He saw the lingering fear in her eyes and knew the process had been an ordeal.

"Why, Mama?" Angel didn't sound pleased. "Why'd you do it?"

"I didn't want to embarrass you. For myself I don't care. I've learned to accept this cross."

"Oh, Mama." Angel moved forward to give her a hug. "I don't care either! Don't feel you have to change for me. But Mama Philena and Cassie have seen you, right? I still don't understand."

"Faye hasn't."

"Faye?" Angel squeaked. "Why should Faye come here?"

"She wrote a letter of apology, though I don't think her mother knows. She said she feels horrible for what her family did to you and me. Of course she was just a child then, and I certainly don't blame her. She's coming for a visit this weekend. Strangely the letter came the same day my friend from New York did." Lila smiled up at the woman who stood by her chair.

"But. . .I still don't understand. Although. . ." Angel grew pensive. "I remember she didn't approve of Rosemary's decision to tell me the truth. She tried to stop it." She sighed. "I always thought that maybe without Rosemary's influence Faye could have been a better person. Of all of them she's the nicest. Still. . ." Her eyes grew fierce with loyalty. "If she can't accept you as you are, she shouldn't be welcome here."

Roland silently agreed. He thought about what Lila had said regarding crosses. They each had one to bear—Angel's being her harsh upbringing and knowledge of her conception; Roland, his gangster family and the blood he could never eradicate; and Lila's cross was living with a man's beard. Oddly enough he realized that, through those crosses, they each had found their strength.

"See there, what did I tell you?" the stranger exclaimed, her accent British with a slight twang. Laugh lines graced her mouth and the corners of her eyes, which were a dark blue and twinkled as they regarded Lila. "You had no cause to fret so."

She set down the foamy straight razor she held, wiped her hand on her skirt, and struck it out toward Angel. "Name's Darcy. Darcy Thomas. And you're Angel." Her smile was as effusive and outgoing as her manner. "I took care of you when you were just a babe in nappies."

Angel laughed at this, shaking the woman's hand. "This is my husband, Roland."

"A pleasure." Darcy shook Roland's hand.

"Likewise."

"Darcy is my oldest and dearest friend," Lila explained. "She gave me a home when I first left the carnival, when Angel was still a baby, and she helped me find my way to God."

"You're the one?" Angel's eyes widened.

"Aye, luv, that I am."

"Oh, we must talk! I have so much I want to know. About Lyons' Refuge that Mother told me so much about, and about how you and she met. . . ."

The gathering moved to the parlor. Over the next hour the women excitedly conversed.

Roland excused himself to take refuge on the porch—women's talk was too hard to follow with their fluttering changes into home, children, husbands, fashion, church, the economy, and whatever else existed under the sun. . .although he never got tired of conversing with Angel.

As the sun set beyond a fringe of distant beech trees, he entered the house for a glass of water. A protesting cry came from the bedroom.

"Oh, that's our boy. Wait till you see him, Darcy!" Angel hurried past Roland with a gentle brush of her hand along his arm, and Darcy beckoned him farther inside.

"You have that hunted animal look my Brent gets when the women sit down for a nice cozy chat." She chuckled in understanding and patted the cushion beside her. "Come, don't be shy. I won't bite. Tell me about the farm and what you do here."

Roland warmed to Darcy's carefree, no-nonsense manner. In a way, she reminded him of Mama Philena, and he found himself opening to her. While he assumed Angel fed the baby, he spoke of his worries—the farm was failing, what with the Depression, and Everett couldn't handle the workload, though he insisted on it. Lila sadly agreed. Roland felt concerned about the health of the man he'd come to consider as both a father and grandfather. "I do all I can, but things are bad. We want to try and keep the farm and not give up on it, as so many other farmers have done. But if we're ever going to manage, we need another hand." He shook his head helplessly.

Darcy got a pensive gleam in her eye. "Well now, guvner, I might be able to help at that. There's a boy at the refuge—well, a man now—been there since I came. Tommy's got a wanderer's spirit, but his clubfoot keeps him homebound. What he doesn't have in stride, he makes up for elsewhere. The boy's as strong as an ox with sturdy arms and build. What would you say if I talked to him and see if he'd be interested in helpin' out?"

"I'd say that would be swell, but I'd have to talk it over with Everett. And. . ." Roland hesitated. "We couldn't pay him. Not with the way things are right now."

"Oh, I imagine he'd be happy enough just for the change of scenery. His two best friends have moved on—Herbert now lives here in Connecticut—that's why I'm here. I was visiting. The other, Joel, well, we've lost track of him I'm afraid, and Tommy's become somewhat restless."

"We have that back storage room we could make up for him," Lila said. "Do ask him, Darcy. I remember Tommy—such a nice boy."

"Now he's a man." Darcy sighed. "Time flies away so fast."

"And here's our little man," Angel announced from behind. "May I introduce you to Everett Roland Piccoli."

She bounced their son in her arms and approached Darcy, who clucked over him. Everett gurgled in contentment, allowing Darcy to hold him.

"Oh, he looks just like his daddy!" Darcy cooed. "What a peach!"

Angel grinned and moved to stand beside Roland's chair; out of habit he slipped his arm about her waist. They shared a look of loving contentment, and Roland wished the room were empty so he could pull her onto his lap and kiss her like he wanted. Their earlier embrace had only whetted his appetite for more.

By the time Darcy left, she and Angel were fast friends. Excited about the prospect of Tommy soon joining them, Lila excused herself to talk to her father. The baby again slept in his bassinet, and Roland did what he'd wanted to do for hours.

He cornered Angel in the kitchen, advancing toward her until he had her back pressed to the wall and his hands around her waist. She gave a soft intake of breath at the unexpected move and wrapped her arms loosely around his neck.

"Roland?"

He kissed her long and thoroughly, amazed that after more than a year of marriage, she still affected his senses as if it was their first time. She clung to him as if she might fall if she were to let go.

He broke away to look into her eyes.

"I don't suppose you really want me to put the coffeepot on?" she whispered.

He smiled at the hopeful note in her voice, his every nerve ending awakened. "I think we should skip that tonight and retire early."

She reached up to brush her lips against his. "I like the way you think, Mr. Piccoli."

"I love everything about you, Mrs. Piccoli."

She gave a contented sigh. "Roland, darling, you can shadow me forever."

He chuckled at her reference to their first days together and kissed her again, thanking God above that his Angel had finally stopped running.